ONE NIGHT, (

At twenty-five, Anastasia Quintin has resigned herself to live in quiet seclusion as companion to Miss Albryght, but one lost wager by her headstrong bookworm of a mistress soon requires Anastasia's return to the society from which she hides. Her first event in eight years is to be a house party in honor of the recently entitled Earl of Huntingdon, hosted by his haughty old grandmother.

Having come to his title by tragedy, the handsome Huntingdon is new to the ton, but he is not new to Anastasia. Dante St. Clair is the very man who long ago stole her heart and thereafter dashed all her hopes and dreams. He is the man she must never let discover her identity, but whom she can no more avoid than a moth can a flame. One waltz will destroy her, and for it, Anastasia will risk everything…and win.

Moll,

Enjoy the Dance!

Alanna Lucas

WISH UPON A WALTZ

An In His Arms Romance

Alanna Lucas

www.BOROUGHSPUBLISHINGGROUP.com

WISH UPON A WALTZ
Copyright © 2015 Alanna Lucas

ISBN 978-1517603-84-7

For Lieke, Ik hou van je kleintje

CONTENTS

WISH UPON A WALTZ

Chapter One

Summer 1822

Anastasia hovered behind Isabel and watched the game of chess progress with dreaded anticipation as she tried to ignore the pain in her feet. When Isabel had agreed to this wager, Anastasia had expressed her displeasure. "Don't worry. I never lose," were Isabel's last words before the game began. It was more than a game of chess to Anastasia—it was a game of chance, and it had already lasted for more than seven hours. Even the sun had given up and retired. It appeared that there was no end in sight.

Or so she thought.

"Checkmate."

"Oh," Isabel gasped. Her hand clutched the edge of the table. "I couldn't have lost. I never lose."

"Well, you *have* lost, my dearest little sister, and now you must pay the price—beginning with the Earl of Huntingdon's house party," Isabel's brother stated with a gloat.

"That was not part of the bargain, Weston," Isabel bleated, disputing the terms of the wager. "We agreed it was to be one season in London."

"No, I said a season *and* parties. A country house party is included in that description."

Philippa, Weston's wife, placed an elegant hand on his shoulder and leaned in close to his ear. "That's enough, darling." Her words were none too soft before her gaze shifted to Isabel, casting a sympathetic look, though her tone bespoke no argument. "One house party before the season begins is not too much to ask. You have rarely been out in society and this is a perfect opportunity."

Anastasia adored Philippa; they had become good friends since she married Weston, but Philippa really was relentless when she set her mind to something. Anastasia truly doubted that Isabel would be able to weasel her way out of this situation.

Dread sank into the pit of Anastasia's stomach. It was still unclear what her role would be if Isabel was to have a season. Over the years, Anastasia had avoided London, and all society for that matter. The nervous anxiety that used to haunt her started percolating, and the cramping in her stomach grew worse. She reached for her necklace only to touch a naked neck; that precious keepsake had been lost to her for eight years.

Isabel leaned back in her chair, crossing her arms. "And when is this *perfect opportunity* to occur?"

"We leave in two days."

Anastasia was uncertain whom the "we" in Philippa's statement included and she was afraid to ask. Isabel, clearly annoyed with her sister-in-law, said in a sharp tone, "We?"

She braced herself for Philippa's response. "You, me, and Anastasia."

"Why doesn't Weston—?" Isabel began to protest only to be silenced by her brother's firm voice.

"I have some unexpected business to attend to, but will join you later in the week." Weston looked up at Anastasia. "Are you unwell?"

She swallowed the hard lump in her throat and tried to sound casual despite her lurching stomach. "I'm quite all right. But why do I need to…?" She started to argue, but Isabel turned around in her seat and looked up at Anastasia with hurt eyes.

"You don't mean to abandon me?"

Anastasia sucked in a deep breath. What choice did she have? It was only because of Isabel's generosity that Anastasia had found a home after being turned away from her family after the scandal. She owed her dearest friend at least one house party. Perhaps Isabel would catch the eye of some intelligent lord and get married before the London season began. Anastasia mentally shook her head. For that to occur, Isabel would have to spend a little more time conversing with the opposite sex and quite a bit less time in the library. Anastasia doubted that Isabel could make a successful match with her head always in a book.

Three sets of eyes stared at her, waiting for her answer. With no other choice, Anastasia resigned herself to the unpleasant fact that she would have to accept. "No, I will not abandon you," Anastasia stated with none of the trepidation she felt.

Isabel jumped out of her chair and wrapped her arms about Anastasia's neck. "Thank you. How would I ever survive without you?"

Weston and Philippa gave Anastasia a knowing look. Isabel *would* be lost without her. They had bonded ten years ago when

Isabel had spent the summer with her aunt, who lived in the same village as Anastasia. After that, the two had become almost inseparable whenever Isabel had visited.

When Anastasia's own family turned her away after the scandal, she had gathered what little belongings she had and asked for a position at Knights Hall. She had hoped to be appointed a maid of some sort, but Isabel had intervened on her behalf, requesting that Anastasia become her companion. Anastasia had insisted that Weston know why her family disowned her, and to this day, he was the only other person beside herself who knew the truth. Weston had promised to keep her secret, and he was a man of his word.

Perhaps this house party was the opportunity that Anastasia was looking for to ease her friend into society. Just because Anastasia's future appeared bleak did not mean that Isabel had to be trapped in the country with her companion. Isabel was young, and should enjoy that youth.

"A country house party it shall be," Philippa exclaimed.

Despite her acquiescence, Isabel was not going to give in to her brother that easy. "I still cannot believe we leave in two days' time. You know very well that I am not fond of crowds and besides, I have nothing to wear and…"

"Not to worry," Philippa's tone was full of mischief. "All that has been taken care of. Lybbe and I even managed to find several costumes for the masquerade in my trunks that Aunt Imogene sent over. Lybbe has already begun some modifications and the gowns will be ready by the time we depart. It is quite fortuitous that the three of us are about the same height and size."

Yes, quite.

"It will be a splendid party." Philippa's enthusiasm was noticeably one-sided.

Anastasia's stomach lurched. She knew Philippa meant well, but she had spent the last eight years avoiding all society. A quiet, mundane life, sequestered in the country suited her better.

"It is only for one week, Isabel. I think you will survive," Weston teased. Her brother was not going to back down.

Philippa chimed in, clearly wanting to ease the tension. "Weston and I agree that you could both do with a change of scenery and the Earl of Huntingdon's house party is the perfect opportunity. Dozens of eligible young men are to be in attendance and I have it on good authority that Lady Huntingdon intends to spare no expense where her grandson's house party is concerned."

Despite all the reassurances, Anastasia was a bundle of nerves. Since moving to Knights Hall, Anastasia had not ventured further than the local village. On the two rare occasions that Isabel did accompany her brother to London, Anastasia had managed to formulate some excuse as to why she could not leave Knights Hall. And Weston did not press the issue. Over the past eight years, he had become a trusted confidant, a brother.

Weston stood and announced, "Now that's all settled, I think it is time to retire."

Before accepting her husband's arm, Philippa came up to her and Isabel. "I know that neither of you are happy about these arrangements, but trust me on this. It will be a wonderful week. One I don't believe you will forget." She ended with a mischievous wink.

Anastasia put her hand on Isabel's arm and squeezed, hoping the subtle gesture would keep Isabel from arguing further this evening. They watched Weston and Philippa leave the room.

The silence lingered on for several moments before Anastasia released her grip on Isabel's arm and walked toward the waning fire, lost in her own thoughts. Anastasia's life was on a different path than Isabel's. There were no seasons to be had or invites to extravagant house parties. No, a quiet country life was all she would ever have now. Anastasia knew the time was nearing when she would no longer be able to reside with Isabel and her family. Life as of late had become too complicated. Everything around her was changing and that scared her.

"I'm sorry. I know how much you detest society and I should not have involved you." Isabel joined her in front of the fireplace. "I should have insisted that you be allowed to stay behind."

As much as Anastasia wanted to agree with Isabel, she could not. She would not desert her dearest friend and let her suffer through a crowded house party.

Even as Anastasia offered a smile of reassurance, her insides writhed in turmoil. "We will get through the next week together."

"I'm not so sure I am going to survive." Although Isabel's words were weighed down with worry, deep down Anastasia wondered if that was just an excuse that Isabel had fabricated so she could focus on reading rather than socializing.

"You will survive, dearest. And besides, a house party is far less troublesome than a season in London. If it becomes too much, we will just go for a long walk."

"I believe I shall be walking a lot in the forthcoming week," Isabel said matter-of-factly.

That plan suited Anastasia as well. With hope, Philippa won't protest too much.

Chapter Two

Dante, the Earl of Huntingdon, stormed through the house, the invitation clutched firmly in his hand. How in the world had he not known what she was up to? He was at his wits' end with his grandmother. Ever since they emerged from mourning, she had been trying to devise a plan to see him out in society and married with all due haste. When Lord Colt handed him the invitation with laughter, Dante left London immediately to confront his grandmother.

"She has gone too far this time," he grumbled under his breath. Without knocking, he entered her private sitting room. The bright pink room momentarily blinded him. "Grandmother, I would like a word with you."

The petite old woman who looked far younger than her three and seventy years put down her book and looked up at Dante. "What on earth are you so upset about?" Her words seemed innocent enough, but the look in her eyes revealed her guilt.

"This." He waved the crumpled invitation in front of her.

"I cannot see what all the fuss is about with you waving your hand like a madman. Hand it to me." Grandmother reached out and snatched the letter from Dante. After a quick glance, she tossed the paper aside and announced, "It appears there is to be a house party."

"Yes, and it is in honor of me. At what point were you going to inform me that"—he paused for a moment and ran his hand through his hair—"hordes of young ladies would be descending on Paradiso in…however many days, all with the assumption that I am in want of a wife."

"Durante," his grandmother said with a sly gentleness, using his given name rather than the nickname that his late grandfather had given him. "I am hosting a house party in your honor." She tilted her head and then with one long diamond-clad finger pointed to the discarded invitation. "And, if you had bothered to read the invite you would have already realized that the guests are due to arrive in two days' time." She glanced over at the gilded mantle clock. "Now, if you will excuse me, Lord Tabard is due to arrive within the next hour."

"No, I will not excuse you." Dante could not believe what he was hearing. He clenched his teeth in an attempt to control his temper, but the smug victorious look on his grandmother's face was his breaking point. "How dare you make arrangements without consulting me?" Ever since his Anna had died, he just hadn't cared what went on in the world around him, and his grandmother had taken full advantage of that grief. It was a problem he intended to rectify beginning with this house party. "I am the Earl of Huntingdon. This is my house, my responsibility now."

Although his tone was harsh, his grandmother's features had not changed. "It is a title you were never intended to inherit. As much as I was displeased with the turn of events when your sainted uncle and cousin died in that carriage accident, and as much as I despair saying so, you are far better suited than they were to hold the title." It was common knowledge throughout the family that Grandmother was fond only of her eldest son and his lone offspring. Despite her deep affection for her now-deceased relatives, she had held genuine concern regarding their ability to run the affairs of the Huntingdon line. Using her position as matriarch of the family allowed her to retain a heavy hand in how the earldom and its holdings were run and how they would be perceived. Nothing was *ever* done without her approval.

"Your confidence in my abilities is most endearing." He had not even attempted to hide the sarcasm from his voice. Dante circled about the room, watching his grandmother calculate her next move. She thought him a pawn on her chessboard. He did not trust her, never had.

"Confidence has nothing to do with it. I will not have this family disgraced by my youngest son or his"—she waved one elegant hand looking for the proper insult—"blackguard of a child who was barely born on the correct side of the sheets."

Dante wanted to defend his cousin but chose to hold his tongue instead. There was no sense in arguing with Grandmother. Many years ago she had declared herself the authority on all topics. Yet, he knew she was plotting something and felt it best to get straight to the point. "What is it that you hope to achieve?"

She stood up and ambled toward him. Although he towered over his grandmother, she was not intimidated by his size. Grandmother had never been intimidated by anyone. "I want you engaged by the end of the week, and married just as soon as all the arrangements could be made."

"I'm surprised that you have not already made those arrangements," Dante growled as he crossed his arms.

"What makes you think I haven't begun? A special license will be easy enough to acquire. All I need is a name." She stepped in closer and looked up into his eyes. Dante saw the hatred and disdain. She had never held any affection for him and never had tried to hide that fact. "On the last evening there is to be a ball. Your engagement will be announced at that time."

"And if I refuse?"

She tilted her head and said in a far too sweet voice, "Let's just say that I can make life extremely uncomfortable for your mother's sister and her daughter."

Rage burned from within. Aunt Ursula and cousin Violet had already suffered enough. He had promised that he would protect them both. When Dante's mother had died when he was just a small child, it was his mother's twin sister, Ursula, who had nurtured and cared for him. He would do anything to protect them and, shrew that she was, his grandmother knew it.

The weight of the title he inherited was nothing compared to the demands that his grandmother had imposed. "Why are you doing this?"

Dante did not think his grandmother intended to answer when she started to walk away from him. Over her shoulder, in a nonchalant tone she stated, "I married your grandfather for his title. He married me for my dowry." She turned around. Her casual manner was replaced with fire and brimstone. "I will not see all that we built thrown away on some inconvenience such as love."

He knew that his grandparents had not been fond of each other, but neither had objected when his father married for love. He started to say as much when the words died and sank into the pit of his stomach as his grandmother's mocking laughter encircled him.

"You think they married for love?" Her harsh laughter jabbed at his heart. "At most they tolerated each other."

It looked as if she was going to say more, but thankfully she held her tongue. Dante did not think he could endure any more revelations today. He did not have any recollections of his parents being together when he was a child, but his father had never said anything untoward about Mother.

"It is my future. I intend to have a say in this."

There was a long thoughtful pause before she answered. "You may choose from any of the women that will be in attendance. I have chosen the guest list carefully. All the women invited have some attribute that would suit the estate and title." She turned and began to walk away. When she reached the threshold, she looked over her shoulder and said, "Do not defy me Durante, or I will make good on my threat."

And with that final warning, his grandmother took her leave.

Damn. Risking his aunt's and cousin's future was not an option.

It appeared he was about to get himself a wife.

Chapter Three

Dante stood at the gallery window and watched as droves of eligible daughters from some of the best families in England descended on Paradiso. Wasn't it ironic? His great-grandfather had built this house as a retreat, a paradise from the turmoil of the outside world, and now it had become a living hell. Dante flexed his hand desperately wanting to hit something. He could no longer stomach the view in front of him. It pained him greatly to see his family legacy reduced to this, a forced marriage to procure an heir.

The servants would be busy with the final preparations, tending to the guests, and delivering the trunks. Dante hoped he could escape to the outdoors through the servants' quarters without notice. Marching out the front door was not option. He turned his back on his duties and headed for the passageway that led to the servants' quarters.

The whole house was a bustle of activity and his break from reality went relatively unseen. Loud sounds of laughter echoed against the peaceful countryside. Dante quickened his pace. He followed the familiar track that bordered the lake and headed toward the conifer woods. A few feet later, a less conspicuous pathway greeted his flight.

The pathway narrowed, the tall trees creating a shady green canopy. Ten minutes later, the outcropping of trees grew sparse and opened to a little garden that framed a small cottage.

Dante went inside and closed the door to the outside world. The familiar scent of paint reached his nostrils and teased his hands. He could not wait to unpack the paints he purchased from the Rowney Company.

If his grandmother knew that he had converted the cottage into his personal atelier, she would probably set the cottage on fire herself. Fortunately, she was not keen on walking in the countryside and had only ventured to the cottage once since it was built. That one visit had ended with her abed with a sprained ankle, causing her to miss most of the season.

The late afternoon had waned, creating a soft, ethereal glow. Dante pulled the cloth off the canvas and admired his latest masterpiece, *Dancing Nymphs*. Inspired by a painting his grandfather had brought back from Italy when he had gone on the Grand Tour in the last century, Dante had fashioned his ethereal beings with abandon. But sitting here now, he did not feel the joy of the dancing nymphs. Instead of reminding him of happier times, as they usually did, today they mocked and laughed at him.

He cast the painting aside and retrieved another that he had begun many years ago. Placing the small canvas on the easel, Dante peered at his subject, wondering what might have been.

The sadness that he had managed to keep at bay had resurfaced as of late. Pulling the necklace from his pocket, he admired the blue and white cameo of a young woman. It always reminded him of the only woman he had ever loved.

Loved and lost.

Dante clutched the precious item in his hand before tucking it back into his pocket. If only she hadn't died. If only he had been able to save her. For eight long years he had mourned her death. Truth be told, he still wasn't ready to let go, but his grandmother's threats were far too severe to be ignored.

Green eyes stared back at him. Struck with inspiration, he grabbed his pad and pencil and began sketching. Within a matter of moments, his ideas came to fruition. The simple lines took the form of a female. He had often imagined her like this, reclined on a velvet settee. She had posed for him once and before he had had the chance to sketch her again, she had been snatched from his life.

* * *

If Anastasia did not know any better, she would have thought that they were travelling to the distant ends of the earth. Problem after problem had only delayed their journey. A simple day-and-a-half carriage ride had turned into three full days. Philippa had sent word ahead that they were to be delayed, but even she was beginning to express her anxiousness at their late arrival.

Philippa glanced out the window while tapping her finger on her lap. "I do hope we arrive before nightfall. It simply would not do to arrive after the evening's entertainments had already begun."

To make matters worse, in between Philippa's worrisome remarks Isabel chattered on about everything she learned of the Earl of Huntingdon's estate, Paradiso. "...And did you know that there is a lake surrounded by classical landscape? The previous earl travelled extensively on the continent and took much inspiration in the Italian style. Weston told me that all the temples and buildings are named to reflect the classical style. Do you think we will be able to take a tour of the estate?"

"I'm sure arrangements could be made," Philippa said as she yawned. "Lord Huntingdon is very amiable."

"Amiable or not, I am most interested in Paradiso. Did you know that there is a tower on the edge of the estate that was built in the first quarter of the last century? The views are supposed to be spectacular."

Anastasia was curious. "How is it that you have so much interest in Paradiso and none regarding the Earl of Huntingdon?"

Isabel shrugged her shoulder, staring into one corner of the carriage. "I'm interested in art and architecture, and things of that nature, not men."

"That might change one day," Philippa said with a giggle.

Although Anastasia's life had not turned out as she had hoped, she did wish that Isabel would find love and happiness. There was nothing more beautiful than the love between a man and a woman. That thought was accompanied by threatening tears. She did not want to think of him, the way he had made her feel, or why he left her. Blinking away the tears and forcing those emotions back into the recesses of her mind, she turned her focus back to her friend.

Isabel's thoughtful stare lingered on. "I suppose one day a man might catch my eye, but he would have to be an exceptional man with an even more exceptional library. He must be kind and honest. Not too tall, but not too short either. I prefer a man who dresses in simple attire. No dandies for me. Oh, and if he detested poetry that would be in his favor."

Laughing at the image that Isabel's description conjured in her mind, Anastasia commented, "That is quite a list. Perhaps we should just wait and see how the week progresses."

"There it is," Isabel breathed out, her nervous energy filling the carriage.

"It's beautiful," Anastasia whispered as she glanced out the window. The impressive lawn seemed to extend for miles before gently giving way to the neo-Palladian façade. The sun had tucked behind the conifer trees, casting various shades of pink into the sky and creating a halo above the magnificent structure.

The extravagance of the privileged never ceased to amaze her. Her own modest childhood home would have easily fit in the portico with room to spare. When she moved to Knights Hall eight years previous, she thought that a spectacular estate, but Paradiso was beyond compare. Awe and intimidation mingled with the anxiety she had been fighting to control for the past several days.

"Is it too late to turn back?" Isabel's voice cracked with emotion, matching Anastasia's own musings.

"Weston has made it clear that he expects you to last the week. I promised him that I would help you," Philippa offered a smile, but Isabel appeared not to notice. "We are in this together."

Isabel eased back on the cushioned seat. She took in a deep breath and whispered out, "I really would have preferred to stay at Knights Hall. I'm just too different from all of them, and when I get nervous I tend to make a fool of myself by spilling something, breaking something, or…"

Reaching across, Anastasia took Isabel's hand in hers. "You have nothing to worry yourself over. Just as Philippa said, we will get through this week together." Anastasia wished she believed her own words. This world that she was entering just seemed too different than the life she had tried to carve out for herself over the past eight years.

Looking out the carriage window, up toward the darkening sky, Anastasia could not shake the feeling that she was being led to her doom. The uneasiness had increased with each passing second for reasons that she could not fathom. She did not know what to make of it, but she tried her best to put on a good face for Isabel and Philippa.

As the carriage came to a stop, efficient footmen were ready to assist. The door opened, revealing a large portico held up by eight columns topped in the Corinthian style. The windows glowed with activity.

Out of the corner of her eye, Anastasia saw Isabel gulp in huge breaths. "If I had any contents to lose, I would lose them right now."

"It will be all right. Once we're settled, you will feel much better. We can have a leisurely evening and be well rested for all the activities tomorrow." Philippa stated before she turned and exited the conveyance.

Isabel eyed her with disbelief.

"I'm sorry, dearest, but we must make the best of our time here." This week was going to be more difficult than Anastasia first assumed.

"Good evening, ladies." Anastasia assumed it was the head butler who greeted them at the base of the steps. The man did not bother to introduce himself. "I have informed Lady Huntingdon of your late arrival." He emphasized the word late before continuing on with his speech. "You will be shown to your room and then may join the others in the Italian room."

They followed the liveried butler up the steps in silence, each casting the other a look of disbelief. Philippa was the daughter of a viscount yet was treated no better than Anastasia, the disgraced daughter of a curate. They had just crossed the threshold into a stark, albeit grand three-story white marble entry hall when a formidable woman dressed in black crepe met them.

"Mrs. Weston, you have arrived at long last. We were beginning to wonder if there was further trouble with your carriage." The constant reminder of their tardiness was wearing thin. It was not as if they had wanted a broken wheel, but some things were out of their control. Obviously Lady Huntingdon did not share Anastasia's viewpoint.

"Good evening, Lady Huntingdon. Allow me introduce my sister-in-law, Miss Albryght, and her companion, Miss Quintin."

Lady Huntingdon nodded in their direction but kept her gaze and attention focused on Philippa. "The week's festivities are well underway. There is to be a masquerade this evening. I do hope you will be able to attend after such a tiring journey." She had uttered the last almost as if she did not believe they experienced such cumbersome delays.

"We look forward to this evening, Lady Huntingdon," Philippa said in a polite tone that was laced with annoyance.

Anastasia could almost read Isabel's thoughts as panic streaked across her face. "Are you all right?" she mouthed.

Isabel shook her head with alarm. But before Anastasia could respond, a middle-aged woman with a scornful scour etched onto her face stepped forward.

"Ah, this is Dabney. She will see to your needs."

Anastasia could not explain why, but there was something about Dabney that did not set well with her. If first impressions were to count for anything, she already did not care for Lord Huntingdon's staff.

"Until tonight." Lady Huntingdon started to walk away, and then, without turning around, she uttered over shoulder, "And please do not be tardy."

The three ladies watched as Lady Huntingdon passed through an archway that presumably led toward the sound of laughter and merriment.

Isabel raised a brow in question. "Amiable?"

Philippa lowered her voice to a mere whisper so that Dabney could not hear her response. "I said Lord Huntingdon was amiable. His grandmother, on the other hand, is quite dreadful."

"Ladies," Dabney called to them.

Philippa pursed her lips shut, the edges rising up in a smile. She had been caught. Anastasia let out a slight giggle when the all too stoic maid glared at her.

"This way." The woman guided them silently through what Anastasia supposed was the guest wing. The size of the wing was deceiving from the outside. The passageway seemed to extend forever, before turning a corner. Large windows allowed the diminishing sunlight to illuminate their way. The house was spectacular. Under different, and more pleasant, circumstances, Anastasia would have loved to explore.

Anastasia gazed on one painting after another of classical Rome. She had wondered how many variations of the same subject matter were displayed at Paradiso. Expecting to see another landscape with ruins in the background, the next painting took her aback. It was of a man, sitting in his study surrounded by books. Several maps were splayed across the desk. Beside him, a window opened up to a view of an Italian landscape. But it was his eyes that she found most alarming. They reminded her of...

"Your rooms are down this last corridor. The staircase at the end leads to the garden room and petit parlor." Dabney's firm voice broke through her pondering.

By the time they reached their rooms, the uneasiness Anastasia had felt during the journey here had only increased. Once they were left alone, she began to address her concerns.

"Is it me or does Lord Huntingdon's staff seem aloof and unwelcoming?"

Isabel put her hand to her chest and sighed out, "Oh, I am relieved you noticed too. I felt as if we were trespassing."

Waving toward the direction of their trunks, Philippa said, "At the very least, the servants are quite efficient. Our trunks have already been delivered."

"Whatever is the matter?" Anastasia glanced over at Isabel, who looked positively terrified.

"Did you not hear? The masquerade is tonight." Isabel plopped down on the sofa, her features forlorn. "There will probably be refreshments."

Anastasia sat beside her and nudged her with her arm, and teased, "I suppose you are quite surprised by the turn of events? What form of monster would invite people to a party and then have the audacity to provide refreshments?"

Isabel shook her head and eyed her with feign contempt. "Isn't it bad enough that I have to be here, but do you really have to tease?"

"I'm sorry, dearest," Anastasia took Isabel's hand. "I'm just trying to help."

"I know and I appreciate it, but I'm just too concerned with causing a scene…again."

Philippa stepped forward and then joined them on the sofa. Her delicate blonde brows were drawn together with concern. "What happened?"

"I have only ever attended two balls in my entire life, and neither went very well. I spilled punch all over Miss Saunders at one and all over myself at the other."

Attempting to lighten the mood, Anastasia teased, "Clearly we must keep refreshments from you." Isabel narrowed her eyes. Trying a different tactic, Anastasia suggested, "You don't have to accept any refreshments."

"I'm most certain that this time will be different," Philippa said with her usual *joie de vivre* attitude.

"True, but then there is the other issue. All the people. I never know what to say. I tend to fade into the background, becoming almost invisible."

"You would rather be noticed and sought after?" This conversation was quickly becoming a battle of wits—one that Anastasia suspected Philippa would win.

"No, not entirely," Isabel pouted. "And besides, I don't like to dance. I would rather play the pianoforte and just watch everyone else. And another thing, I have never been asked to dance."

Anastasia and Philippa glanced from one another as understanding dawned on both of them. Isabel had never danced with a man, and was most likely scared. Before Anastasia could ease her mind, Isabel crossed her arms and firmly stated, "I will not go."

Anastasia would have to address one problem at a time. "You have to. Lady Huntingdon is expecting you to attend."

"You can go for me." Isabel's eyes brightened with the mischievous look she had learned from Philippa.

"That is a wonderful idea," Philippa chimed in a little too enthusiastically. She went to one of the trunks and began pulling garments from it.

"Lybbe is going to be quite distressed when she sees what a disaster you are creating," Isabel playfully scolded her sister-in-law, all semblances of her worries from a few moments ago having gone by the wayside.

Pulling out an elaborate and far too exquisite dress for Anastasia, Philippa announced, "Here it is." Philippa held up the dress that had been designated for Isabel. "I know you don't care for green, but think how your eyes will stand out."

"You will look lovely in my dress," Isabel commented, a wide smile gracing her features.

"Isabel, *dearest*, I really do not believe it a wise idea for me to pretend to be you, even if it were only for one evening. And besides, it isn't proper to pretend to be someone I am not."

Philippa gave her an incredulous glance. "You are not really pretending to be Isabel. You are just not being yourself. It is a masquerade, and no one is who they say they are. Everyone needs a little adventure in life." She ended her lecture with that same mischievous smile Isabel displayed just a moment ago.

Once upon a time, Anastasia would have agreed with Philippa.

"Please, I promise not to put up a fuss for the rest of the week if you will go to the masquerade tonight." If Isabel were the type, she would have batted her eyelashes at that point.

"And what do you intend to do while I am parading around as you?"

"Read, of course."

"I don't know. What if Lady Huntingdon discovers that we switched places...?"

"Nonsense, how is she going to find out? I will be there." Philippa was not going to back down. "*If* Lady Huntingdon does begin to suspect, I will distract her and you can hide yourself away. And besides, a night of frivolous entertainment where no one will recognize you is just what you need."

Shaking her head, Anastasia directed her retort to Philippa, not even trying to disguise the sarcasm, "I am *so* relieved that you have figured out what I needed."

"I am not going to argue with you. Isabel and I insist that you attend and that is final. Now, let's get you dressed."

Anastasia knew she would not win this argument. When Philippa set her mind to something, no one was safe. "Fine," she harrumphed. "I will wear Isabel's costume."

"Thank you," Isabel said as she came up and hugged Anastasia. "I know that you will have a wonderful time. You won't regret this."

She already had.

* * *

With Lybbe's assistance, and Isabel's commentary, Anastasia and Philippa had dressed for the masquerade. As discussed, once Philippa was ready, she left for the ballroom ahead of Anastasia while Lybbe completed the final touches. Philippa had thought it best that she arrived first, engage Lady Huntingdon in conversation, thus providing a distraction for Anastasia.

Anastasia looked at herself in the mirror, hardly recognizing the woman who was staring back at her. She was not used to wearing fancy clothes. Tilting her head, she admired the elaborate hairstyle. Lybbe had even managed to weave some silver ribbon through her hair.

She was actually getting excited. She had never attended a masquerade before and this would be her first *and* last.

Isabel walked up with the ornamented mask in hand. "Time to put this on."

Anastasia held the blue and green creation with silver scalloped edges in place as Lybbe tied the ribbon in back. The moment the mask was in place, it was if she became another person. A sense of freedom that she had long thought dead bubbled within. It was as if she were seventeen again and the world held so many promises.

"You are so beautiful," Isabel said over Anastasia's shoulder. Anastasia noticed tears welling in Isabel's eyes before she turned away. The thought brought a smile to her face. Isabel was not as composed as she always tried to appear.

"Thank you, dearest."

"Now, off you go. I will wait up for you and Philippa." Isabel ushered her to the door with haste. "Have fun," Isabel whispered with excitement as Anastasia left the room.

Anastasia wandered through the vast house, making her way to the ballroom. There were no other guests in sight. She must have tarried longer than she thought. She was so nervous that she imagined that if she opened her mouth, the butterflies fluttering in her stomach might escape.

This was insane. She was insane.

She shouldn't be here. What did she hope to achieve by dressing up and attending the masquerade? *One night to be free. One night to pretend.*

It had been so long since she gave into such diversions. Perhaps one night was possible. One night to lose herself in everything that she had wanted and could not have. She leaned over the marble balustrade and watched the dancing couples below. Fanciful plumes glided over elegant ladies. Pinks, blues, and greens mingled in the sea of costumes. An intoxicated black and white domino whisked through the crowd bumping into several ladies, causing a ruckus. A beautiful young woman clad all in white waltzed through the vibrant colors, reminding Anastasia of sea foam brushing the shore.

"Oh, how I wish I could have had just one more dance with him," she murmured under her breath. "I know we could have been happy together."

Anastasia blinked away the tears. She had the rest of her life to dwell on what could have been, what she hoped her future would have been like. Tonight was for giving into her folly, her desire, one night to forget the past and live in the present.

Before she changed her mind, Anastasia pushed away from the banister and hurried toward the grand ballroom. At any moment, she suspected the guards would interrupt her flight of fancy and take her away to Bedlam.

A lively tune greeted her as she neared the ballroom. There was a lightness in her step and a sway in her soul. Anastasia could not remember the last time she danced.

An image flashed through her mind of a young couple waltzing endlessly through a shady copse. Laughter filled the air followed by a sweet first kiss. Despite everything that had happened, she longed for his kiss and the way he made her insides flutter.

So lost in her own musings, Anastasia had not realized that the music had stopped, nor that all eyes were upon her. Thankful for the mask that hid her features, she glided down the steps into the warm room hoping to disappear without further attention into the sea of costumes.

Lavender, lilac, rose, vanilla, and several other unknown odors assaulted her senses. She edged her way from the crowded area, hoping to find a quiet spot to recover when out of the corner of her eye, she saw Lady Huntingdon push her way through the crush of people.

Anastasia's first thought was to run. Lady Huntingdon could not discover that she and Isabel had switched places. The excited butterflies had turned into treacherous locusts threatening to destroy her. She had to leave. Anastasia turned, and bumped into a man dressed all in black, including his mask which covered most of his face. Warm brown eyes glistened in the candlelight, inviting her into his world.

"May I have this dance?"

Anastasia's mouth went dry. She knew that voice. The heartache that had been lingering for years burst into flames.

Chapter Four

Dante looked about the room, wondering how long he would have to endure this masquerade before he could sneak off to his study and enjoy a quiet evening alone. He detested his new role as the Earl of Huntingdon.

Surveying the guests, he spotted Lady Brenda who, although quite beautiful in an elaborate white gown, did not attempt to hide her identity. He watched her move through the crowd of guests. Everyone seemed to naturally flock toward her. She was exceptionally comely, but there was something about her that he did not trust. He suspected that underneath her sweet façade laid a woman who would do anything to get what she wants. Dante chuckled inwardly; Lady Brenda reminded him of his grandmother and a woman such as that was not for him.

Somehow he had avoided dancing thus far, but with Lady Brenda approaching on the heels of his grandmother, Dante suspected his luck was about to change. He searched for a means to escape when from across the room he spied her. The unknown siren was draped in a deep green gown. Her mask of blue, green, and silver illuminated her eyes. The very essence of the masked beauty drew him closer. Who was she?

Even from this distance, he could sense that she was nervous—flustered even. Dante walked toward her with one intention.

"May I have this dance?"

She did not answer, but accepted his hand. An unexpected jolt surged through his body the moment their gloved hands touched. They moved in time to the rhythm of the waltz. The masked siren formed perfectly to him.

Swirling through the ballroom, whiffs of lavender and vanilla encircled him. It was a common enough fragrance amongst the ladies of the *ton*, but this, this was different. *Honey*. The faint sweetness of honey wafted through the air. He breathed in the intoxicating mixture. Without thought, he let out a sigh.

"Is anything the matter?" The masked siren whispered out as he led her through another turn.

"No, you just remind me of someone from a long time ago."

"Someone you loved?"

Her question caught him off guard. His eyes met hers, but she glanced away. "Why do say that?" How could she see his inner thoughts after only a few minutes of dancing when he hardly knew himself anymore?

"I hear the sadness in your words."

When he did not answer her question, she plagued him with another. "What happened?"

There was a long pause.

What could he say? "She died." The two words spilled from his mouth without thought.

The lady missed a stepped and fumbled against him. He caught her and held her close. His body instantly reacted. "Who are you?" He said as he glanced down into her beautiful green eyes.

She did not answer. He had no clue as to who this woman might be, and before he could discover her identity, she struggled out of his grasp, pushing him away with force. Her brows were creased together in a sort of paranoid confusion. She reminded him of a caged animal trying to escape.

It all happened so quickly. One moment they were dancing, and in the next, she was pushing her way through the crowd of onlookers. Dante reached for her, but was blocked by the crush. Straining to see over the tops of elaborate hairstyles, he watched her run straight through the open veranda doors and disappear into the night.

Dante had to go after her, discover who she was. He had barely moved five feet when his grandmother halted him. "Let her go. Do not cause more of a scene."

That was all his grandmother had ever cared about, appearances. Dante met her cold gaze. "I must see if the young lady is unwell." He did not wait for his grandmother's reply.

Shouldering his way through the guests, he edged his way toward the open doors. Once clear of the masqueraders, he picked up his pace and ran onto the veranda. The dark landscape consumed all that was around. There was not a soul in sight. Dante made his way down the steps, but a silver ribbon caught his attention. Bending down, he picked up a mask. It was the same his mysterious dance partner was wearing.

Who is she?

* * *

He didn't know who she was.

He thought she was dead.

"Dead," Anastasia cried into the night. She had not stopped running until she reached the temple. She rested her head against the cold, fluted column, pounding her hand over and over against the unforgiving stone. Pain ricocheted through her hand, but she didn't care. It didn't matter. Nothing mattered. What was he even doing here?

Anastasia knew exactly what he was doing here. While she had been rotting in her grief, Dante—no, she mustn't think of him as the man she once loved—Mr. St. Clair had been living this extravagant life filled with parties and soirees. He had been happy and joyful, probably quite the rake about town while she was banished from her family in shame. If not for Weston and Isabel, she probably would have died. There were days when she wished she had.

"He didn't even know me." Rubbing her head against the column. A jagged sigh escaped her mouth, "He didn't even know me." The pain in her chest was almost unbearable.

What was she going to do? It was not like she could just leave. She had no means of her own. What was she going to tell Philippa and Isabel?

Nothing.

Anastasia could run away. She could leave her home at Knights Hall, leave Isabel and everyone she had come to care about. She could escape to some dark corner where no one would find her.

The warmth drained from her body and a heavy ache settled in her limbs. She was drowning in grief and tired of avoiding people for the fear of someone discovering what she had done. Why should she alone bear the weight of that mistake? Had she not suffered enough? Her family had been cruel, had sent her away. Perhaps they had told Dante that she was dead, but why?

Reason was edging into her thoughts. Although life had not turned out the way she thought it would, she *was* part of a family now, a family who cared about her, and she did not want to lose them.

None of this made any sense to her. Even if her family had told him that she was dead, she had sent dozens of letters before being sent away. Why hadn't he answered them? Why does he deserve happiness and she does not? One night, one mistake and her whole life had changed. She pushed off the stone column, her hands clutched at her sides. She wanted answers.

Trying to determine her next course of action, she paced the length of the temple portico. She did not know what to do or how to proceed. Closing her eyes, she inhaled the cool night air.

Anastasia could not go on alone. There was only one thing she could do. She would have to reveal her past to Philippa and Isabel. She only hoped that their opinion of her would not change for the worse.

With that settled in her mind, it was time to retreat back to her room. There was one problem, though: the masquerade. She was unsure how to reenter the house without being seen. And then a thought occurred to her.

Anastasia made her way back toward the house, hoping not to encounter anyone. As she neared, she watched and waited for the stroke of midnight when the masks would be removed, revealing everyone's identity. She hoped that Mr. St. Clair would be amongst those waiting to take off their masks and not searching for her. She would then sneak back up to her room. It was a simple plan in theory but fraught with problems.

The veranda doors were still open, allowing the faint sound of music to waft through the summer night. A sudden cool wind sent a shiver down her spine. It was nearing midnight. The couples looked like they were moving toward the center of the ballroom.

Sliding against the balustrade, she edged up the veranda steps, and stopped behind a large marble urn and peered around. The masked guests had congregated at the center of the ballroom, waiting for the stroke of midnight. With haste, Anastasia moved around the urn and continued ascending the stairs. She kept to the darker parts of the veranda, hopefully out of sight.

After surveying her surroundings, she determined which opening she must enter through in order to go unseen. Slinking inside the ballroom, she kept herself concealed by a large portly woman who was commenting to her neighbor about how handsome Lord Huntingdon looked this evening. Not being able to resist the curiosity, Anastasia stretched her neck, but to no avail. She had yet to meet, let alone see the elusive new Earl of Huntingdon. Balancing on her tiptoes, Anastasia tried to catch another glimpse, but a tall, broad-shouldered man blocked her view.

Deciding it was best to keep to her original plan, she eased back toward the wall and kept her head down. When she heard the call to remove masks, she picked up her pace. This was her chance. While everyone was intrigued with who was who, she could make her final escape.

The moment she saw the masks begin to come off, she practically ran toward the passageway that she hoped led to her room. Anastasia bumped into several people, but only offered a quick apology and kept running.

By the time she reached her room she was so out of breath, she thought to tarry a bit in the hall before entering her room, but the sound of voices getting closer caused her to reevaluate that plan. She hoped that Isabel was not waiting up for her. She was not up to revealing her secrets to Isabel tonight.

Anastasia gently turned the knob and opened the door that led to their adjoining sitting room, and then with the same amount of caution closed it, careful not to make a sound. She slinked to her room and slid inside. Anastasia didn't know how she managed it, but somehow she was able to undress herself. However, she was most certain that the dress would need mending.

* * *

Dark shadows danced across the muted walls. For one brief moment, a glimmer of light streaked across, scaring the shadows away, then like all the joy in her life, grew smaller and smaller until once again darkness ruled.

Anastasia ripped the covers off her and stormed to the windows. She could not open the window quickly enough. She was suffocating under her own sadness. She fought for air, consumed by sobs. Her fingers fumbled with the latch before she was able to open the window. Cool air rushed across her wet, hot face, but it offered no relief to the inner turmoil boiling inside. She inhaled deeply, taking in the sweet country air.

Moonlight danced across the landscape, reminding her of a bygone time when two lovers had snuck into an abandoned cottage and proclaimed their love.

Stop! Her mind screamed its demand. *Stop torturing yourself.* He didn't know her. How could he not know her? She had forbidden those thoughts from manifesting for eight years and they *had* acquiesced, until one dance brought it all back.

The painting she saw when she first arrived not only stirred those feelings, but also made them worse. He looked so similar to the man in the painting. Could Dante really be related the Earl of Huntingdon? She searched her memory, hoping for some recollection or clue. Nothing came to mind. She really did not know if he *was* related to this family or not. After all that they had shared, wouldn't he have said something about being related to an earl?

Images of their brief time together danced through her mind. It had been the most wonderful year of her life. She remembered the first day they met as if it were yesterday.

The days had shortened and the wind had turned cold, but for the first time in over a week, there was not a cloud in the sky. Anastasia remembered that she was supposed to be helping her brother. Previous lashings from her father when he had discovered her disobedience had been sealed in her mind forever, but she could not resist the clear blue sky or the beautiful scenery. It was too nice of a day to be cooped up indoors. She snuck out the back door of their modest home. Her father had asked not to be disturbed while he prepared his sermon. At least she knew that her brother would not be able to tattle on her right away.

Anastasia ran from the house with only one destination in mind. By the time she reached the old abandoned cottage, she was out of breath and giggling with her successful flight. She glanced at that old structure with fondness. One day she wanted to live there. It was in the most perfect location. A large oak shaded it from the summer sun, while a little stream careened around it in the near distance.

Her father had caught her playing there when she was a child and forbade her to ever return. When she questioned why, he scolded her something terribly in front of her siblings. After that humiliation, she never asked again. Her eldest brother had told her that they used to live in that cottage, but after Mother passed away they left and never returned. Anastasia knew the reason why. It was her fault. Everyone blamed her for Mother's death, but how was a newborn baby responsible for that?

"One day," she sighed out, lost in her own thoughts.

"One day what?"

Anastasia whipped around and came face to face with most handsome man she had ever seen. His eyes were like sipping chocolate, warm and inviting.

The word squeaked out. "Nothing." She cleared her throat, attempting to sound more like a woman than a mouse. "It's…I plan to live here someday," she had managed to say with pride.

The handsome stranger peered around her. He cringed, clearly noticing the dilapidated state of the structure. Anastasia's dignity dwindled. She thought he would tease, so when he spoke his next words, it came as quite a shock. "I think it would make a lovely home." Then he smiled at her and at that moment she knew her world had changed forever.

Too overcome with the new sensations fluttering through her, Anastasia scurried off. She had not even learned his name. That night, so upset, she cried herself to sleep.

The next day had proved to be the worst day of her life, up to that point at least. The torrential rain had prohibited her from journeying out, and worse still, her father was so furious for the previous day's folly that he had given her extra chores.

By the following day, the rain had stopped, but the sky was still grey. Anastasia knew it was silly to believe that the handsome stranger would appear again, but as soon as her morning chores were complete, she had hurried to the cottage.

Over the years, she had attempted to keep the cottage in the best repair she could. She had spent many hours cleaning it and dreaming of her future. Her heart sank as she neared. He was nowhere to be seen. Feeling disheartened, she walked up the overgrown path and opened the rickety front door that was in need of replacement.

Anastasia stopped short. The table in the small foyer had been uncovered. A simple white vase filled with wildflowers stood proudly in the center. Did someone break in? Her heart pounded, but then reason questioned. Why would a stranger break into an old cottage and bring fresh flowers? Her imagination was really getting the better of her.

Reaching for her necklace, she fingered the cameo. It had been her mother's. It was the only keepsake she had been given, or rather taken from her mother's trunk that had been left to rot in the attic.

"Is anyone here?" she called out.

A figure emerged from what was supposed to be a sitting room. Anastasia jumped back and was about to run for her life when sunlight streamed into the small space revealing…her stranger.

"I didn't mean to frighten you." He strolled toward her. He was quite tall, and even more handsome than she remembered from just two days ago. "It's just you left in such a hurry the other day, I didn't have the opportunity to introduce myself."

Anastasia was paralyzed, not with fear, but with another, entirely different and unfamiliar feeling. She watched as he moved closer, unable, and simply not wanting to move. Perhaps she should be frightened or at least a little wary, but she was not.

He bowed in front of her. Lifting his gaze, his brown eyes met hers. "Dante St. Clair, at your service, my lady."

Anastasia's world had brightened that day, and for many days after, until…

An owl hooting in the distance, the wind rustling through the trees, all sounds from the living world brought her back to her lonely present. Anastasia blinked several times.

"Dante," she whispered into the night, hoping that the wind would carry her troubles far away. Hot tears stormed down her cheeks. She was tired of being strong, tired of always trying to hide her emotions.

Not tonight.

Clutching the drapes, she gave into the heartache and cried.

Chapter Five

Isabel glanced over the top of her book. "I was wondering if you were ever going to wake. I want to hear all about last night." She looked lovely sitting serenely in an apple-green day dress. Guilt struck Anastasia. She had dressed for the day in the hope that Isabel and Philippa would have left already to join the others. Although she had resolved to tell them her secret, doubt had crept up and settled on her shoulders.

Despite her own insecurities, Anastasia was never one to take her own woes out on anyone else; she responded with whatever cheer she could muster. Trying to delay the inevitable, she said, "My head…" She began rubbing her temples, attempting to make her lie convincing, and added, "I guess I just needed some sleep."

"I wish I had slept better." It was unlike Isabel to have difficulty sleeping. Anastasia was just about to ask what was the matter was when Isabel volunteered. "I kept hearing strange noises during the night, almost like crying."

"Perhaps you were dreaming." Anastasia's curt response earned her a glare from Isabel.

"But I was wide awake."

Thankfully Philippa entered the room, the awkwardness from the moment before dissipated under Philippa's cheerful voice. "Wasn't the masquerade splendid?" She raised a quizzical brow at Anastasia. "Where did you disappear to last night?" Her tone was light until their eyes met. "What's wrong?"

"What happened?" Two sets of concerned eyes held her in place.

"I need to tell you something." Anastasia broke away from their questioning eyes and went to sit on the settee beside Isabel. Philippa joined them, lowering herself daintily into the damask chair beside Anastasia.

"You are positively trembling." Isabel reached out to clasp her hands. "Your hands are like ice. What happened? You're scaring me, Anastasia." Isabel's brow crinkled.

Guilt sank in the pit of Anastasia's stomach. She had always feared that if Isabel learned the truth about her scandal that she would send her away, too shocked and embarrassed. The silence dragged on while she contemplated what she wanted to say.

"Please, you can tell me anything." Isabel squeezed her hands. "You are like a sister to me."

Anastasia did not know where to start.

Philippa leaned in and placed her hands on top of Isabel's. "Sisters tell each other everything," she said with a soothing smile.

Their reassuring words, smiles, and genuine concern gave Anastasia the confidence she needed to share her story. She inhaled deeply and prepared herself. "More than eight years ago I met a young man who had been visiting his aunt near the village where I lived with my father and siblings."

Isabel interrupted. "Is that the young man who broke your heart? Is he...?"

Anastasia had only ever said that her heart had been broken, nothing more. "Please, let me finish without interruptions and then I promise I will answer your questions." She was certain that if she hadn't asked Isabel to wait, she would have continued to bombard Anastasia with questions, and, she feared, any interruption would cause her to break down and not finish her story. "Very well, but I *will* have questions."

Anastasia was most certain Isabel would.

"Where was I?"

Philippa squeezed her hands, clearly trying to move the story along. "Visiting his aunt."

"Oh, yes. We started spending time together, and I fell in love." Anastasia shook her head. "Before you interrupt, yes, he did break my heart. I thought he loved me the way that I loved him. After he went away I wrote to him, but he never answered my letters. I was sent away shortly after that and you know the rest."

Philippa's brows crinkled with confusion. "I still don't understand why you were sent away unless... Oh my." She offered Anastasia a sympathetic smile. "I am sorry you had to endure such ill treatment. I know what it is like to be deceived. Why didn't you ever say anything?"

"I assumed Weston told you when you married."

"He never said a word, but I suspected something dreadful must have happened." If only Philippa knew all of it. No, it was better that she did not. Weston was the only other person who knew what led to her final downfall.

Bewilderment crept over Isabel's face. "Your father sent you away because…you and this young man were…?" A blush streaked across her face. She cleared her voice. "But why?" The tone in her voice suggested that she did not quite believe the story. It was true, there was just one detail missing. They were the closest of friends, but there were just some things she did not discuss.

"My father was the curate and afraid of scandal." She hoped that snippet of truth would pacify Isabel's curiosity.

"Why are you telling us this now?"

"I was too embarrassed to tell you sooner and did not want to hurt your feelings, or be sent away." She had kept this secret and the worries along with it locked inside for far too long.

"I could never send you away." Isabel squeezed her hand to emphasize her point.

Anastasia realized that she did not want to hide in some dark corner of the world embarrassed and ashamed. She may not ever marry, but she had the love of her friends, and that was just as precious.

"I still don't…" Philippa stopped as realization dawned on her. "Oh my. He's here."

"It is worse than that."

"How could it be worse?"

"I danced with him last night, and he did not recognize me." The more she said the words, the worse it hurt. "Then he told me that he thought I was dead. Of course he said this not knowing he was saying it to me, because…"

Isabel reached over and gave her a hug. "I am sorry you have to endure this." She sat back and let out a loud sigh. "What are we going to do?"

"Discover why he believes that Anastasia is dead." Philippa turned to Anastasia with an apologetic smile. "I'm sorry, that sounds dreadfully morbid."

Anastasia shook her head. "It is quite all right. How do you propose to uncover that information?"

Philippa was silent for the longest time before a wide grin appeared. "You were pretending to be Isabel last night, so Isabel will pretend that it *was* her last night."

The space between Isabel's brows crinkled. "So I am to pretend to be me, pretending to be you, and now it *is* me trying to discover information about you. I'm utterly confused. I have a difficult enough time just being me and now you want me to pretend it is but it isn't me? I don't see how this is to accomplish anything."

By the consistent rambling, Anastasia knew Isabel to be nervous about the entire pretense, and she could not blame her. Pretending to be someone she wasn't was exactly why Isabel had not wanted a season in the first place. Fancy dresses, endless entertainment, and constantly trying to impress was not in Isabel's vocabulary. Anastasia would not have asked for help if she didn't feel so hopelessly lost.

"Please, I need you. I just need to know why he never returned my letters, why he made empty promises, why he…" Anastasia was about to reveal too much. That was one secret she would not reveal, not to her dearest friends, not to anyone.

"It will only be for a few days," Philippa reasoned.

Isabel inhaled a long deep breath then exhaled slowly. "Fine, I'll help."

Philippa was positively giddy. "Just think of the fun we will have with this subterfuge."

Ever since Philippa entered their lives, nothing had been mundane and ordinary. She brought a certain *joie de vivre* that had been missing in all their lives. Philippa stood and paced in front of the unlit fireplace, deep in thought.

"How are you thinking we should progress?" Now that Isabel had agreed, she appeared eager to participate.

Philippa did not answer. Biting her lower lip, she squinted into the distance, shaking her head. Without warning, she clasped her hands together and turned to face them. "Afternoon tea is to be served in the garden. That would be the perfect opportunity. Isabel, you will try and entice…" Philippa's attention turned to Anastasia's. "Who is it that we are to hoodwink?"

Just the thought of saying his name to someone else caused her insides to somersault. She swallowed hard. "Mr. St. Clair."

Philippa gave her a peculiar look. "Dante St. Clair?"

Anastasia's head snapped up. "You know him?"

* * *

Yes, Philippa knew him. He was a good friend of her cousin, Marcus. She did not doubt Anastasia's story, but it did not make any sense. She knew that the now former Mr. St. Clair had suffered a tremendous loss. Could that be what this was about?

The longer she remained silent the faster her heart started to beat. Philippa did not want to lie, but needed to discover more information before she revealed her friendship with him to Anastasia. Thinking quick, she settled on a half-truth. "I met him at Aunt Lou's, oh, it has been…" Philippa shrugged her shoulders, feigning forgetfulness over how many years it had been.

Isabel gave her a quizzical look before she launched into a series of questions. "When was the last time you saw him, Philippa? Did he ever mention Anastasia?" Isabel had the look of amateur investigator. Clearly she had been listening to Weston regarding his investigations over the years for far too long.

"No, Isabel." Anastasia's face grew long, the sorrow deepened in her eyes. Philippa wanted to ease that pain. "But, it is also a topic of discussion not appropriate for him to discuss with a relative stranger."

That statement seemed to ease some of Anastasia's angst.

"How are we to proceed?" Isabel's question was a reminder to Philippa that Isabel was a novice in almost everything, especially social intercourse. They best get this done and over with before Isabel came to her logical senses.

Philippa turned to Anastasia. "What exactly happened last night? We need to know every word that was exchanged, everywhere you went, everything."

"I told him that he looked sad. He told me that I reminded him of someone that was dead. I stumbled while dancing and then ran out the veranda door."

"That was all?" It was such a brief encounter; no wonder Philippa missed the entire episode. Regardless of length, it seemed to have caused Anastasia a tremendous amount of distress. "Is there anything else that you want to tell me?"

Philippa could not help but wonder what secret Anastasia was harboring. She would write to her husband, tell him what has transpired, and ask him to arrive sooner. Only Weston knew the entire story. Philippa could not explain why, but something about the situation did not sit well with her.

Anastasia looked nervously about before she declared with a shaky voice. "No, I have told you everything you need to know."

Philippa was familiar with that phrase. Weston had tried to protect Philippa far too often by not revealing all. She would allow Anastasia to get over the shock of seeing her lost love before pressing for more answers.

"Very well." Turning to Isabel, Philippa dictated the next course of action. "We will attend the afternoon garden party. You will need to speak with Lo…" She cleared her throat, "Mr. St. Clair away from Lady Huntingdon."

Oh, I should not have said that, Philippa scolded herself. Not surprisingly, Isabel was the first to question. "What does Lady Huntingdon have to do with Mr. St. Clair?"

Philippa was not going to dance around the truth any more than she needed. "They are related."

Anastasia's hand flew to her mouth, as a loud gasp exited. "From the moment I met her, I felt there was…something."

"Don't you worry. Isabel and I will do our best to glean the information you seek. I think it wise that you stay here this afternoon."

Anastasia nodded her head. "Of course, I will read or sew or…"

"She will probably pace a rut in the carpet," Isabel teased before her tone turned serious. "We need to go now, before I change my mind."

Philippa needed a just a moment to scribble a quick note to Weston. Fifteen minutes later Philippa and Isabel were ready for their grand performance.

"We will return to rescue you from boredom in a couple of hours," Philippa said as she closed the door. Anastasia did not say a word but offered a sad sort of smile. Philippa was determined to set things right. She just knew there was more to the story than met the eye.

They almost reached the end of the hall when Isabel finally spoke what was on her mind. "Why do I get the impression that you are more acquainted with Mr. St. Clair than you stated?"

Philippa answered her in a hushed tone. "Because I am. Anastasia's Mr. St. Clair is the Earl of Huntingdon."

"No!" Isabel gasped. "How…?"

Philippa raised her hand to silence Isabel. She thought she heard footsteps from around the corner. Better to be safe than to have rumors spread throughout the countryside. "That is correct," Philippa began in a loud voice, "The previous Lord Huntingdon added this wing so that he may entertain on a much grander scale."

They had just rounded the corner when they almost collided with Lady Huntingdon.

"Oh, I do apologize, Lady Huntingdon." Philippa could not help but wonder if the noise she heard had in fact been Lady Huntingdon eavesdropping. "Miss Albryght and I were just admiring…"

"Yes, yes, I heard your rather loud explanation." Well, that assumption was confirmed. "I see that you are missing someone in your party."

Isabel quickly responded. "Miss Quintin took ill shortly after we arrived. She has been abed ever since."

"Oh dear, I hope that it is not severe?" Lady Huntingdon did not conceal her artificial concern.

"Actually, Miss Quintin was suffering throughout our journey here. All the motion and delays did not sit well with her." Philippa hoped that by exaggerating Anastasia's supposed ailments Lady Huntingdon would not probe further.

Pursing her lips together, Lady Huntingdon eyed them both for the longest time before she finally stated, "I hope her health improves. Now," she snickered, "tea is about to be served shortly and we do not want to be tardy."

Lady Huntingdon turned and walked toward the staircase. Philippa assumed by her curt statement that they were expected to follow.

* * *

Dante's grandmother had planned an eventful day. After tea and refreshments were served, there were to be lawn games. He had learnt that morning that his grandmother had expected him to sit next to the winner of the competition at dinner this evening. He knew the afternoon was contrived so that his grandmother's first choice would be the victor, and he had no intention of bowing to all of his grandmother's demands. He would join the ladies for an hour then retreat to his study. There were far more important matters to contend with than his grandmother's matchmaking schemes.

Dante was listening to Lord Tabard with half an ear over his latest improvements to his estate. He knew the man was in the marriage mart, but his boisterous declaration about how much money he had and was willing to spend would only land him with a fortune hunter. Of course, Lord Tabard was perhaps one of the most disagreeable men he knew and buying a woman's affections may be the only way for him to secure a bride. It would not be the first time something of this sort had happened.

Gazing across the lawn toward the house, a late arrival caught his attention. From this distance it looked to be…no, it couldn't. His heart started to pound in his ears, further blocking the sound of Lord Tabard. As the young woman neared, Dante knew it was not whom he was first suspecting, but where could that woman be?

With the approaching ladies, Lord Tabard decided it was the opportune time to excuse himself to a more venturous task. "I believe I shall seek out Lady Brenda."

Dante gave him a sideways glance. He wanted to encourage the old lord in his endeavors. If Lord Tabard married Lady Brenda that was one less woman that his grandmother could thrust his way. "She is walking near the footbridge."

As Lord Tabard waddled away, Mrs. Weston and her companion strolled up toward his table. Now at a closer glance, and despite her similar features, Dante was certain that the woman at Mrs. Weston's side was not his mysterious lady from last night.

Dante stood and greeted his guest. "Good afternoon, Mrs. Weston."

"There was a time when you called me Philippa," she returned with a smile.

"Yes, that was before I inherited this title." Dante leaned in and lowered his voice, "And before my grandmother lurked behind every tree and corner."

Philippa let out a hearty laugh. "Yes, I quite understand." She extended a hand toward the woman beside her. "I do not believe that you have met my sister-in-law, Miss Albryght."

"How do you do, Miss Albryght?"

"Pleased to formally make your acquaintance." A silent understanding seemed to pass between Miss Albryght and Mrs. Weston before she continued. "I enjoyed our dance last evening."

Miss Albryght couldn't be his masked siren, Dante was certain of it. However, he did suspect that she knew more than she was willing to admit.

"So you have met my grandson, Miss Albryght?" The sound of his grandmother's voice heightened his caution. What was she up to now?

Miss Albryght looked as if she was a fox trapped by a hound. "Yes," she swallowed hard. "La…last night…"

Regardless of who she was or who he thought she wasn't, Dante would not subject Miss Albryght to his grandmother's interrogation.

"Miss Albryght, would you care to take a turn about the garden?"

Again, Miss Albryght looked to Mrs. Weston for guidance. "I'm sure Miss Albryght would enjoy a turn about the garden. I believe I will stay here and converse with Lady Huntingdon. I am keen to learn her itinerary for the season."

Dante had no clue as to what Mrs. Weston was about but was thankful nonetheless. He didn't want his grandmother near while he tried to determine what Miss Albryght knew about the woman he danced with at the masquerade.

Miss Albryght worried her gloved fingers and bit her bottom lip. Dante attempted to ease her nervousness. "I apologize for my grandmother."

"No need. But thank you just the same. Your estate is quite lovely. Do you have any plans for improvements? My sister-in-law told me that each of the Earls of Huntingdon did some sort of improvement. I suppose it was part of their legacy."

Dante did not know when Miss Albryght would stop her questioning. Not wanting her to faint from lack of air, he interjected, "No, I hadn't really thought about improvements." When they entered the garden, the fragrant scent of roses mingled with the sweet air took him back to a distant time and place. Without thought he uttered, "I was not expecting to inherit."

"Why ever not?"

It took a moment for Dante to realize what he had said aloud. Since the tragedy was no great secret, he said, "My uncle and his only son died in a carriage accident and now the responsibility has passed to me."

"You do not sound happy about the change of events."

"I would have preferred to remain unmarried, but now that I am an earl, my grandmother has other ideas in mind." Dante did not know why he was revealing so many confidences, but despite Miss Albryght's initial nervousness, she was quite easy to converse with.

"Is that why you were sad last night?"

"What did you say?"

"Last night, when we danced," she paused for a moment as if she was having difficulty speaking. "I commented on your sadness."

This *was* the woman he danced with last night? But it couldn't be. Last night the masked lady entranced him. He felt an instant connection, and although he found Miss Albryght pleasant, there was no reaction.

He realized that he had not said a word in quite a few seconds. "I do apologize; I seem to have forgotten myself."

"Not at all." Miss Albryght opened and closed her mouth as if she were going to speak.

The cravat around Dante's neck seemed tight and restrictive all of a sudden. He needed to be away from here, away from this conversation. All his assumptions had been incorrect?

"Thank you for the stimulating walk. I believe it is time we joined the others." Without further word, he escorted Miss Albryght back to where some of the other guests were gathered, bowed and took his leave. He did not want to socialize or converse with anyone, especially his grandmother.

* * *

Isabel did not know what to make of their conversation in the garden. She had done everything that Philippa had suggested, but Lord Huntingdon seemed agitated and distant when she mentioned the dance. Despite her best efforts, she was not very good at subterfuge, she thought with a sigh.

She glanced about for Philippa, but was punished with the sight of Lady Huntingdon approaching her with a determined purpose. Instantly, her nerves began to get the better of her. Thank goodness her gloves hid her sweaty palms.

"Miss Albryght, a word please." Lady Huntingdon did not wait for a response but strolled away from neighboring guests, expecting Isabel to follow, which she did. She scolded herself inwardly. If she were to survive a season in London, she best become more forceful. "I want to know what was exchanged between you and my grandson. He is quite discomposed over your brief encounter."

Lady Huntingdon's harsh stare bore into Isabel. If she were the crying sort, she would be sobbing uncontrollably. Swallowing hard, she said, "We talked about the estate. I am quite fond of neo-classical architecture."

"What else?" Her impatience was making Isabel even more nervous if that were possible.

"I...I asked if he had any plans for improvements." Lady Huntingdon gave Isabel a look like she expected her to explain further, but there really was nothing else to say. "That was all," she said with all honesty. Lord Huntingdon gazing off into the distance was hardly worth mentioning.

Lady Huntingdon eyed her for several seconds before she seemed satisfied with her answer. "Very well, you may rejoin the others." Her tone was firm. Clearly, she was used to giving orders.

The moment Lady Huntingdon left her side Philippa came scurrying over. "What was all that about?"

Isabel placed a trembling hand at her chest. "She questioned me about my stroll with Lord Huntingdon. She did not seem at all pleased."

"We best return to Anastasia."

Chapter Six

Dante was thankful estate business had pulled him away from the afternoon's activities his grandmother had planned. He was still fuming about her underhanded tactics. After he finished with his steward, there was still plenty of time to join the others, but all he wanted was peace and quiet. The library afforded him the opportunity to regain his senses and think about the problem at hand.

He was certain that Miss Albryght was not the masked woman with whom he had danced last night, regardless of her having knowledge of their conversation. True, she looked similar to that woman, but when she placed her hand on his arm as they took a turn about the garden, the spark he had experienced last night was not there.

And then there were her questions. For reasons he could not explain, her questions had unsettled him. Images of Anna had flashed before him. Did he miss her that much that he could conjure her out of thin air? No. Something was not right. The woman he danced with last night was real. He had her mask to prove it.

Grandmother was another source of contention. She had been most eager to point out that the week was well underway and he had yet to pay attention to any one lady in particular. Her threat hung over him like a boulder about to crush him. He had been avoiding this decision. Eight years ago he was prepared for marriage, but when Anna died, part of him died too. He had resigned himself to the fact that he would remain a bachelor. He had been content with that decision, but now that he was the family's titled earl, it was no longer his decision to make.

Miss Saunders was an agreeable young woman, he thought to himself as he closed the book and paced the length of the room, but her high-pitched voice made the hairs on his neck stand on ends. Then there was Lady Brenda, his grandmother's first choice. She was accomplished in music and art, could speak French and Italian. Her manners were impeccable, her lineage impressive. There was only one problem. There was no connection. He felt nothing.

He strolled over to the window and looked out over the lush green landscape dotted with violet orchids. *Violet.* Much as he hated the old woman, and the situation in which he found himself, he couldn't refuse his grandmother, not with his cousin's fate hanging in the wind.

Dante was doing this for Violet and Aunt Ursula. He closed his eyes and rubbed the bridge of his nose. This was such a disaster. How had his life become so complicated? He opened his eyes, his vision obstructed by the fingers still pressing firmly to his head.

Movement in the distance caught his attention. His hands dropped to his side. He squinted his eyes to get a clearer look.

Three women were walking in the direction of the folly, their backs toward the house. One looked to be Mrs. Weston, and the other to be Miss Albryght, but the third, dressed in sky blue, was unfamiliar to him. Dante clutched the window frame. With each breath he took he became more lightheaded. It couldn't be her. He knew it couldn't be her. She was dead.

He tried to focus on the direction the trio was headed, but his heart demanded his attention, pounding in his chest with remembrance. The woman clad in blue turned. Her face was in profile, but her smile touched his heart. Lightning coursed through his veins, bringing his body back to life.

He began to back away from the window, intent on following her. He turned to go after her when Gibbs entered the library.

"Excuse me, Lord Huntingdon, your grandmother wanted me to inform you that the ladies shall be returning shortly and your presence will be required in the music room."

Dante struggled to find words. "Th-thank you," was all he managed to choke out. Gibbs absented himself without another word, leaving Dante to relive one of the darkest moments in his life.

He slumped down in the leather chair, the coolness surrounding him. He rested his head back and closed his eyes. For many years now, he had not allowed himself to think of the day he learned that Anna had died.

That distant day had started with excitement and anticipation. He had finally worked up the courage to tell his grandparents about the woman he loved. His grandmother had accused Anna of being a fortune hunter, but Dante had assured her that it was not the case. He had never revealed who his family was. At that time it didn't appear to be significant; he was third in line to inherit. His grandfather was still alive. His eldest uncle and his son were all hale. Little had Dante realized all the turmoil that lay on the horizon.

Grandfather had been more understanding of the situation. He wouldn't give his blessing until he met Anna, but Dante knew that as soon as his grandfather met her, he would love her just as much as Dante did.

He remembered the long journey to Plymouth. Although it had only taken five days from London, it seemed to take months. He had thought about visiting his aunt beforehand, but he was too impatient. He needed to see his Anna. Dante remembered how nervous he was when he walked up the pathway that led to her father's house. He had rehearsed his speech a dozen times.

The moment the door opened, he knew his world had changed forever, and not for the better.

"Who are you?" A young man clad in mourning clothes and no older than Dante demanded.

"I am Mr. St. Clair. I have come to see Miss Quintin."

"She's dead," the man replied curtly as he tried to slam the door on Dante.

Dante must have misheard him. "What?"

"Who's come to visit?" An older man said as he pulled the door open. "What do you want?" He had never met or even seen Anna's father, but he assumed this to be him. They had the same green eyes and reddish-brown hair.

"Mr. Quintin? I've come to inquire after your youngest daughter."

The man's face was long with sorrow. "I regret to inform you that my daughter passed away two weeks ago."

What happened after that, Dante was unsure. Somehow he managed to make his way to Aunt Ursula's house, which was less than a ten-mile journey. For days afterward he could barely eat, too consumed in his own private hell to care about anything around him. His aunt and cousin had watched over him, cared for him.

"She's dead," he had repeated over and over. "I can't believe she is gone."

"I'm so sorry, Dante," his aunt said.

"They didn't even tell me what happened."

"Violet learned that she died in an accident on the way to visit her aunt." Aunt Ursula rubbed a gentle hand through his hair. "I'm so sorry..."

Laughter rang through the entry hall, bringing Dante back into the present. He shook his head, trying to erase those painful memories.

The sounds of merriment grew closer. He was in no condition to be host to a party of cheerful women. Instead of entertaining and socializing, he would retreat to the only place he could ever find any relief from the demands that now plagued him. He would lose himself in painting. It was the only balm that had soothed his soul.

Without further thought, Dante stood and made his way to his usual escape route.

* * *

"Where is my grandson?" Dante could hear his grandmother's demanding voice echo through the family wing. He had hoped to avoid seeing her until after dinner, but it would seem that luck was not on his side.

"Good evening, Grandmother," he said as he entered her private sitting room, forcing a polite tone.

Rather than return the greeting, his grandmother went straight into one of her lectures. "You are an earl now and duty requires you to be present and to entertain your guests."

"They aren't my guests—they are your guests."

"Do I need to remind you of our bargain?"

You mean threat, don't you?

"Lady Brenda was inquiring after you. I believe she would make an excellent countess."

Dante would not have this conversation. "I still have time to decide."

Grandmother approached him and sniffed the air in a most unladylike fashion that he was sure she never exhibited in front of anyone else. "Where exactly have you been all afternoon?"

He decided to answer her, but he would not discuss what she believed was best for his future. "I had business to tend to, and then I took a long walk."

"You've been painting again."

"Yes." Dante was tired of hiding his passion for painting and sketching. Events may have forced him into this new role, but it didn't mean that he had to give up part of himself.

"How many times have I told you that I disapprove of that so-called talent of yours? It is positively shameful."

"Grandfather did not think so. In fact he had often encouraged me to…"

"Well, he is dead and I don't want you wasting your time on such frivolities when there are far more important pursuits to be had."

Feeling bolder than he had in years, he retorted, "Like courting a woman that I do not love."

Her voice rose. "Like doing your duty!" Grandmother's face had turned an unflattering shade of red. "Remember what we discussed. I would hate for your aunt or cousin to suffer because of your selfish nature."

Dante was fuming. He could not believe his own grandmother would resort to such threats. She was the one who was selfish. Dante shook his head. This was not going to end well if he stayed much longer. Through gritted teeth, he muttered, "I must go and change before dinner."

* * *

The next day had proved to be no better. There had been one emergency after another that needed his attention. Dante knew with time, he would become more fluid dealing with all the estate business, but at the moment he grappled with certain aspects of a large working manor.

After his business concluded, Dante should have been a proper host and gone hunting with the other men, but being proper was furthest from his thoughts at the moment. What he wanted to do was discover who the mysterious masked siren was and why she had toyed with his heartstrings.

He glanced up at the clock on the mantel. It *was* too early to imbibe. His head and heart demanded relief from the events of last night's dinner. To prove her point, his grandmother had done everything in her power to keep him and Lady Brenda paired for the entire evening. Every time he had tried to speak with Mrs. Weston or Miss Albryght she would waylay him like a wolf pack leader. He had spent the better part of the evening with his jaw clenched tight, attempting to stamp down the angry words that burned his throat.

Even now, the frustration was steadily growing. Pain shot through his jaw as he clenched his teeth. He had to stop this. He pushed the ledger to one side, pulled out his drawing supplies from his desk drawer and then stared longingly at the blank page. With each breath he took, images of his Anna danced in his head.

Dante pushed away from the desk and strolled to the window. A warm breeze whipped around him, drawing his attention to the lush green lawn in the distance. A female figure was practically running away from the house. Although he could not see her face, he knew by the way she moved it was his masked lady.

What was she running from? What was she up to? All the ladies were supposed to be in the grand parlor taking tea, and yet she was running in the opposite direction.

Careful to not be seen, Dante left his study, pretending to have business on the estate. Once clear of the entry hall, he picked up his pace to a full run. If his grandmother had known that he was skirting his duties yet again, she would have a heart attack.

Dante ran in the direction of the copse. His masked lady's flight was easily concealed amongst conifer woods. He followed the trail that ran along the perimeter of the meadow but could not find the mysterious woman. Perhaps she had taken one of the side pathways that led away from the meadow. Dante would not stop until he discovered where she had gone.

* * *

The moment Anastasia saw Mr. St. Clair running down the trail, her heart skipped a beat. Too many conflicting emotions were vying for her attention. Not wanting to be seen by him, she ran off the trail and quickly hid amongst the thick outcropping of trees. Once he passed, she made her way back toward the manor, steering clear of the trail.

This had not been a good idea, she scolded herself as she scurried toward the house. When Philippa told her that the ladies were gathering for tea then cards, Anastasia had thought it would be the perfect opportunity to enjoy the spectacular summer day that reminded her of those cherished times from her carefree youth. She was tired of being cooped up in her room.

By the time she reached the portico, Anastasia thought she had out maneuvered Mr. St. Clair. She had just entered the foyer, when the sound of her shoes clicking softly on the white marble floor was disrupted by the sound of her name echoing through the elegant space.

"Anna, wait."

"Damn," she muttered the unladylike word. Anastasia turned around, but refused to look at him, instead keeping her gaze settled on the pristine white marble floor. This was the moment she had been dreading. She would not give him the satisfaction of knowing her.

With caution, he approached her. "It is you," she heard him sigh with relief. "Anna, where…?"

Anastasia raised her eyes to his. She saw the pain and despair in his eyes. *Good.* She steeled her nerves. He would not crush her hopes and dreams beneath fairy tale promises. She had to stay strong. "I'm sorry to have to correct you Mr. St. Clair, but my name is not Anna." She had not been called by that name in over eight years. That person no longer existed; like he had said, she was dead.

Confusion streaked across his face. He took a hesitant step toward her and began to extend his hand almost as if he intended to touch her. Did he think her a ghost?

She backed up several steps. Anastasia fumbled for words. "I best be returning to my friends."

"Wait," he pleaded. He continued to gaze at her, to look deep into her eyes, searching. Anastasia knew she should walk—no, run—away, but she couldn't. The longer he stared, the faster her heat beat. "Please, Anna."

"For the last time," she said with all the frustration that was brewing inside, "I am not Anna. That woman is dead." She blinked quickly trying to fight back the tears. She would not let him see her cry. Anastasia turned to run from the room and almost collided with Gibbs.

"Pardon me, Lord Huntingdon. Lady Huntingdon has requested Miss Quintin's presence in the south parlor."

Anastasia whipped around and stared at him. *Lord Huntingdon?* Dante St. Clair was the Earl of Huntingdon. Her world started to spin, humiliation the catalyst. Is that why he claimed he thought her dead, so that he would not be ashamed by her lowly station?

The moment Gibbs said her name she could feel Dante's eyes bear down on her. There would be no denying who she was now. She swallowed hard, still refusing to make eye contact with Dante.

"Good day L–lord Huntingdon." She spat the words from her mouth as if they were poison. Anastasia could not walk fast enough. She practically ran from the room with Gibbs following close behind her. There was no escape, or anywhere to run and hide. All she wanted to do was withdraw to her room, pack her things, and sneak away.

As she neared the parlor the high-pitched laughter of Miss Saunders rattled through the delicate space. Slowing her steps, she inhaled deeply, attempting to catch her breath. It wouldn't do to arrive all out of sorts. Lady Huntingdon already did not care for her, and she had to think of Isabel's future. She would not do anything to bring disapproval to Isabel and ruin her chances for a good season.

"This way, Miss Quintin." Gibbs appeared to be a dutiful servant, but his air of superiority was quite unnerving. Even though she was a guest, his attitude toward her was barely civil. She had no idea what she had done to earn such scorn. She could not concern herself with that now, not when she was about to walk into the lion's den.

By the time Anastasia entered the parlor her nerves were quite undone. She had to remind herself to breathe. Those pesky butterflies threatened to discompose her when all she wished was that they would simply carry her away to a distant place.

The ladies were gathered for a game of whist. Anastasia spotted Isabel at a far table, where thankfully there was an empty chair. Keeping her focus on the empty seat, she meandered through the grouping of elegant ladies who turned down their noses at her as she passed. Anastasia was within several feet of her destination when a firm voice dictated a change of course.

"We have an empty seat available, Miss Quintin. No sense in being shy, please come and sit with us." Although her words appeared kind, the tone in Lady Huntingdon's voice was full of contempt.

Anastasia took the seat beside Miss Saunders and watched the game of whist that was already in progress.

"Are you enjoying your stay?" Miss Saunders inquired in a voice that sounded more like that of a child than a full-grown woman.

Keeping her reply short and praying for no further questions, Anastasia said, "Yes, and you?"

"Very much so," Miss Saunders said as she placed card down on the table.

Anastasia watched with feigned interest. She was no card player and really had no clue as to what this game was about.

"Do you reside with Miss Albryght, Miss Quintin?" Lady Huntingdon inquired. Anastasia suspected that an inquisition was forthcoming. She tried to continue to keep her answers brief and nonchalant. "Yes."

"Miss Albryght is such a dear and so intelligent," Miss Saunders chimed in, clearly oblivious to Lady Huntingdon's motives, whatever they might be.

"And how long have you resided at Knights Hall, Miss Quintin?" Lady Huntingdon clearly had a goal in mind.

"Eight years."

"And do you not have any plans to marry?" My, Lady Huntingdon was being direct. Anastasia could feel Philippa's sympathetic gaze soothe her from across the room. If it weren't improper and rude, she was certain that Philippa would have rushed to her side the moment Lady Huntingdon's interrogation began.

"No." Anastasia could see another question forming on Lady Huntingdon's lips. She could only endure so much. "I have no intentions of marrying." The other women present at her table leaned in close as if she were to reveal some dark and enticing secret. All that she hoped to accomplish was to satisfy Lady Huntingdon's curiosity and to squelch any possible rumors. "Not now, not ever."

Lady Huntingdon appeared quite pleased by that statement, but still eyed her with circumspection. Anastasia wasn't attempting to be deceitful. What she said *was* true. She had had her heart broken once and was not prepared to risk it again.

By the time the games concluded, the last thing Anastasia wanted to do was dress for dinner. She did not want to see Lord Huntingdon or put on any pretense. All she wanted to do was cry, but even that would have to wait.

"You look quite lovely this evening, Isabel." She was wearing a pistachio evening dress ornamented in the French style. The color embellished her green eyes.

Isabel looked up at Anastasia with puzzlement. "You are not dressed?"

"I am feeling rather tired this evening and…"

"What's wrong?" Isabel knew her all too well for Anastasia to hide her true feelings for long.

Without guard, the words spewed from her mouth in a sarcastic tone that was barely civil. "Oh, besides being cornered by Lady Huntingdon all afternoon? I'm sorry," she quickly relented as a frustrated breath filled the air about her. She wanted to scream or throw something or…punch Lord Huntingdon, née Mr. St. Clair.

"What happened?" Without reserve, Isabel came up to Anastasia and took her into a sisterly embrace.

Isabel and Philippa knew the truth—well, most of it—about her and Lord Huntingdon, so why should she try and conceal what eventually will be made known? These were her friends, her family, and she needed them more than she could have ever realized.

"He knows I'm here." She stepped out of Isabel's warm and safe embrace. Anastasia turned to Philippa, not even attempting to hide the hurt from her voice. "Why didn't you tell me St. Clair was the new Earl of Huntingdon?"

Guilt and remorse streaked across Philippa's face. She came up to Anastasia and took her hands in hers. "I promise you that I did not know before yesterday that the man who broke your heart was one and the same."

The tears, just like those pesky butterflies, were going to be her undoing. "But why, why didn't you say…?"

Philippa spoke up with haste, "I don't believe he ever meant to cause you harm."

"He looked at me as if I were a ghost."

"Did you say anything to him?"

Anastasia nodded. "I denied who I was, and I wasn't very kind to him."

"What else happened?"

"Nothing. Gibbs interrupted and confirmed my identity. After that I left and joined the ladies." Anastasia whipped around clutching the fabric of her dress. "And to make matters worse Lady Huntingdon would not stop questioning me about my intentions."

"Your intentions?" The look on Philippa's face was almost comical. "I had wondered what she was saying to you, but from where I sat, I could not hear a word. That was not what I was expecting to hear."

"Yes, well, I suppose I am not worthy of her illustrious house party." Anastasia did not care if the sarcasm offended her friends.

"Now that you know who Lord Huntingdon is, what are you going to do?"

The question hung in the air.

Never in Anastasia's wildest nightmares would she had ever thought that she would come face to face with the man who had hurt her more than her father had when he sent her away. Her intentions used to be clear, but being here so close to him only served to destroy her assumptions and muddle her thoughts.

"I don't know."

"Don't worry about this evening." Isabel came up to her. "We will not leave your side."

Chapter Seven

Dante left the earl's suite with a single purpose in mind; to speak with Anna. But no sooner had he ventured twenty feet into the hallway, his grandmother appeared from her private sitting room.

"A word with you." His grandmother's tone bespoke no time for argument, but Dante was not likely to oblige for too long this evening. He followed her into the room. The moment he entered the pink sitting room, the smell of peppermint assaulted his senses. He would always detest that smell.

He stood waiting for her to speak, not even attempting to hide his annoyance with her.

She sat perched on the edge of her seat, her posture perfectly vertical with the back of the chair. She had been a master at making him wait; dragging out the simplest discussion just to prove that she was in control.

"I hope you remember our agreement." She pulled one delicate glove on her liver-spotted hand and then glanced up at him, narrowing her eyes, contemplating whether he understood.

"How could I forget?"

She smiled, clearly pleased with herself. "Excellent." She began to pull on the other glove. "You may go."

Dante would not give her the satisfaction of the last word. "I hope *you* remember that the choice of wife is mine. I will choose from any of the ladies in attendance." His words had clearly struck a chord with her. He was playing with fire, but it was a chance he was willing to take to have Anna at his side.

Having made his final statement, he left the room, leaving his grandmother to stew in her own ultimatum.

* * *

As guests filled into the Italian room, Dante held his breath in nervous anticipation. When Gibbs had said her name, confirming her identity, he wanted to pull Anna into his embrace and rekindle what had been lost, but too many questions stood in their way. Anger and disappointment coiled through him like a snake about to strike. Why would her family tell him that she was dead?

"You look like you intend to kill someone," his longtime friend Lord Colt said as he approached.

Dante was in no mood for idle talk. "I might have to," he eyed his friend.

"What is the matter with you? Ever since you discovered that Lady Huntingdon had planned this house party you have been a volcano waiting to erupt." His friend's analogy was apropos. He had been dormant these past eight years and at any moment he felt like he would explode.

Running a hand through his hair, he turned to Colt and leaned close. "Do you remember the young lady who I had intended to marry eight years ago?"

"The one who died? Yes, you were a bloody mess for months." Colt began to laugh. "Don't tell me you are seeing ghosts again?" Colt had been his closest friend since he was a lad, had seen him through some of the darkest hours of his life, but he did not always have a way with words.

Dante shook his head. "Not ghosts, but the woman in the flesh and blood."

Colt met his gaze, clearly stunned by what Dante had said. "But I thought her father told you she was dead."

"He did, but I met her this afternoon."

He shook his head in a double take, confusion wrinkling his features. "Where?"

"Here, in my house." Dante could see the wheels turning in his friend's mind. "No, I don't believe she is here to extort or blackmail."

"You never know," he said with that sinister tone he had acquired after his own would-be fiancée had accused him of getting her with child and then abandoning her for another. Fortunate for Colt, the lady in question's scheme was revealed before too much damage was done.

"She denied who she was and wanted nothing to do with me. And besides, Anna was not like that." No, she was the most caring, honest woman he had ever met.

"Then how do you know it really is her?"

His patience was dangling by a thread, but he supposed he owed his closest friend some sort of explanation. "As we were arguing over her identity, Gibbs came into the room and said her name. It is her."

"Did she explain why she was suddenly back from the dead and attending your grandmother's house party?"

"No, she ran off." Dante watched as another small group of guests entered the room. "But, I intend to get to the bottom of this tonight." He would wait all night if needs be, even if he had to follow her to her room.

* * *

When Anastasia entered the Italian room with Philippa and Isabel by her side, all eyes seemed to turn toward them, but Anastasia felt the heat of the stares specifically on her. Her pulse was in competition with her heartbeat. Although she felt lightheaded, somehow she managed to make it to the nearest empty sofa without causing a scene. All propriety set aside, she plopped down and held her hand to her head, hoping that by the time she looked up, everyone would have found a new interest.

"Are you all right?" Philippa whispered from the seat beside her.

Anastasia could not even think clearly enough to form two words. From across the room she spied Lord Huntingdon eyeing her. She could have handled this evening much better if he weren't present. She knew that at some point during the evening, he was going to corner her and ask questions. Some for which she would not have answers. She still could not comprehend why her family told him that she had died.

"Do you want to retreat?" Isabel questioned.

"No." If only the firmness of her word was a match for the anxiety lurching within. If she had survived for this long, she could muster the energy to endure the house party. It was not like she could stay locked in her room until it was all over.

The trio sat on the settee in quiet contemplation. Philippa had the look of a woman who was about to scheme. Anastasia leaned in and in a hushed tone scolded, "I do hope that you are not plotting anything."

Philippa's eyes rounded with a *Who, me?* look. Anastasia was all too familiar with that look. It usually meant that Philippa *was* concocting some sort of scheme. "Please," Anastasia began in her most pleading tone, "I beg you not to intervene."

"I would not do anything that would bring any harm or embarrassment to you." Philippa patted her hand. "Trust me."

Anastasia did trust Philippa, but was still worried that she would play matchmaker. If Weston were here, he would agree. His wife had a knack for such craftiness. As if sensing that Anastasia might tell her so, Philippa excused herself to go and speak with Lady Lamden.

"I wish this evening was already at an end." Isabel worried her hands in her lap. She appeared just as nervous as Anastasia, but for entirely different reasons.

"I know," Anastasia said as she offered a sympathetic look. "It will get easier with time." She was not going to remind Isabel how hectic the London season would be, but she wanted to offer words of encouragement. "And besides…" Her words died off as the room suddenly quieted.

Without even glancing in the direction of the opening, Anastasia knew who had just entered the room. The dread in the pit of her stomach was slowly forcing its way up her throat. She truly detested the way that woman made her feel. After several deep breaths and some incoherent reassurance from Isabel, Anastasia turned toward where everyone was glancing.

Lady Huntingdon made her grand entrance. Clad in black, she looked like death with her pale features and large biscuit-colored eyes. She settled a harsh gaze on Anastasia. A shiver ran down her spine and Anastasia had to fight the urge to get up and run from the room. She wished that somebody, anybody, would distract Lady Huntingdon from her target.

Help came from an unlikely source. "Grandmother," Lord Huntingdon began as he stepped in front his grandmother, blocking her view of Anastasia, "Lady Brenda and Lady Mathilda were most curious about your recent holiday in Bath." He did not give his grandmother the opportunity to speak, but guided her toward a group across the room, where Anastasia presumed the ladies in question were sitting. He glanced over his shoulder and gave Anastasia a sympathetic nod and reassuring smile.

Her body stilled, but those butterflies began to wreak havoc with her insides. She demanded her eyes glance away from Lord

Huntingdon. She did not want to remember his dashing smile, or the way he made her knees weak with just a simple glance, and she definitely did not want to remember how his lips felt on her.

Warmth flooded her senses. The room seemed to close in about them. She could not draw her gaze away from his. He held her captive with those mesmerizing eyes. She swallowed hard, fumbling to open her fan.

"Miss Quintin, you look positively discombobulated," Miss Saunders stated in her usual high-pitched squeak, which served to break the spell that Lord Huntingdon had over her. "Perhaps you would enjoy a turn on the veranda."

"Yes," she somehow managed to utter out between waves of her fan. "I believe I would enjoy some fresh air." With more energy than she thought possible, Anastasia practically jumped off the settee. "Isabel, will you join us?"

Isabel really did not need any encouragement to escape the crowded room. Within a matter of moments, the three women had emerged into the cool night air. Isabel kept to herself, gazing across the moonlit landscape. Anastasia knew her dearest friend was longing for the quiet solitude of Knights Hall just as much as she.

"It is so pleasant here in the country," Miss Saunders said as she went to the elegant balustrade.

"It is indeed. Do you not spend much time in the country, Miss Saunders?" Anastasia had always assumed that most only went to town during the season.

"No, most of my time is spent in London or Bath." She gestured toward the shimmering lake. "Oh, but look how the moonlight plays upon the water. I would never leave if I had views such as this."

Anastasia agreed with those sentiments. Paradiso was a splendid estate with all sorts of diversions. Any woman would be most fortunate to live in a setting such as this. It was a sobering thought. One of the ladies inside would be the next countess with *him* at her side. Anastasia turned away, hoping the darkness concealed her dismay.

"I've never been to Bath," Isabel began as she guided Miss Saunders back toward the door.

"Oh, it is quite a lovely place. I prefer it much more than London." Miss Saunders continued to ramble about why she preferred Bath, giving Anastasia plenty of time to regain her composure.

When she approached the pair, Miss Saunders turned her attention back to Anastasia. "You look much recovered, Miss Quintin."

"I am, thank you."

Miss Saunders smiled sweetly, the deep dimples lighting up the dim veranda. She really was one of the most thoughtful ladies she had ever met. She embraced Anastasia's arm and said with much excitement, "I am glad to have met you. I hope you do not think me forward, but I feel a certain connection with you."

Anastasia had noticed it too. This was not the only time that Miss Saunders had come to her rescue. It was nice to have friends that didn't judge.

"I feel the same."

Dinner was announced and the three walked in silence back into the Italian room. Philippa, Isabel, Miss Saunders, and Anastasia were all misfits in some way. Anastasia felt a certain camaraderie with her new friend.

Everyone partnered and filed into line. Anastasia knew that she would be the last to enter the dining hall. Holding her head high, she took her place beside Mr. Bacon. The man was eager, too eager in her opinion, to make her acquaintance.

"Lady Huntingdon has informed me that you are companion to Miss Albryght."

"Yes, for the past eight years." She detested this part of the evening, when she would be forced to make polite conversation.

"And you reside with Mr. and Mrs. Weston."

"Yes, that is correct." She shifted impatiently from one foot to the other, wondering how long they would be made to stand and wait.

"And I suppose that when Miss Albryght marries, you will seek a new position?"

Anastasia had not thought much about what would happen after Isabel married. She supposed she could not expect to be her companion forever.

Changes—too many changes. Not for the first time that evening had Anastasia wanted to run from the room and hide under the bedcovers like she used to when she was a little girl, frightened by thunder.

So lost in her thoughts, she did not hear Mr. Bacon until he repeated, "I say, Miss Quintin, don't you agree?"

She had no clue as to what the man was referring to, so she simply smiled and nodded.

"I knew we were of the same mind." His loud boisterous laugh echoed through the room, causing those around them, including Lord Huntingdon, to stare.

The couples paraded into the great dining hall with all the pomp and elegance expected from those who came from wealth and position. It was a scene from her childhood imagination. Only in those scenes, everyone was happy and pleasant, unlike most of the guests present, who only seemed to be putting on airs for Lady Huntingdon's exclusive benefit. Anastasia longed for the leisurely, informal dinners at Knights Hall.

From the other end of the table, Anastasia could feel the heat of Lord Huntingdon's gaze upon her. She did not know how much more she could handle in one evening.

"Would you care for buttered prawns?"

She blinked her eyes several times, trying to focus on the meal and not the way Lord Huntingdon made her feel.

"Yes, thank you, Mr. Bacon." Her words were barely audible even to her own ears.

Despite how hard she tried to focus on the meal and the conversation that swirled around her, Anastasia continued to lose herself to thoughts of him. Why did he think her dead? Why had he never returned her letters? Why…?

"You are awfully quiet, Miss Quintin." She did not know how long she had been lost in her musings, but Mr. Bacon's intrusion and subsequent scold reminded her that she was on display.

"I do apologize; I fear that I am not myself this evening."

With an air of superiority, Mr. Bacon leaned back in his chair, rubbed his excessive belly and declared, "I believe an evening of rest is in order."

This was the only comment of his with which she agreed. Anastasia had already formulated her plan for escape.

* * *

All bloody evening he had wanted to talk to her. She had offered artificial smiles to Mr. Bacon and incoherent responses while gazing at her half-eaten plate of food. He knew her to be uncomfortable and there was nothing he could to do to aid her. He was furious with his grandmother for the way she glared at Anna when she first entered the Italian room. He may not understand what was going on or why she suddenly appeared at this house party, but Anna did not deserve his grandmother's contempt.

Throughout dinner Anna had looked like she wanted nothing more than to escape. Every time he glanced at her, she had the look of someone deep in contemplation. He knew how she felt. He could not escape thoughts of her. Dammit, he wanted answers. He glanced over at Colt who offered a half smile that barely concealed his amusement at the current situation.

By the time dinner had ended, Dante was in a foul mood. The ladies had retreated to the music room while the men went to the library. He didn't want to join the men, but at least he was away from his grandmother's calculating interventions, allowing him time to think. How could he protect his aunt and cousin, discover the truth about the past, and thwart his grandmother's schemes?

Words from his most recent visit with his aunt rushed to the forefront of his mind: "Don't let Lady Huntingdon's own wants come at a sacrifice to yours. You deserve happiness. And don't worry about us; we can rise above the gossip. It wouldn't be the first time."

He had spent his entire life crushed beneath the weight of his grandmother's demands and it would end tonight. He had a second chance with the woman he loved within his reach. If he could not speak to Anna alone, he would enlist others to aid him. Mrs. Weston and Miss Albryght were the keys to help him unlock the past.

It seemed like days had passed while waiting for the appropriate time to rejoin the ladies. Dante tried to be a good host, but based on the teasing sneers from Colt, his attempt was not successful.

When he entered the room, he scanned it, hoping to find Anna alone. Not only had he not seen her alone, he had not seen her at all, and to make matters worse, his grandmother was approaching with Lady Brenda at her side.

"Lady Brenda has informed me that she is quite an accomplished singer, and when I told her that you played the piano forte, well, we both agreed that a duet was in order."

Based on Lady Brenda's red-stained cheeks, Dante suspected that she had never said anything of the sort. "Perhaps you would care to take a turn about the room instead?"

Grandmother seemed most pleased by his gesture, but his reasons were entirely his own. He had noticed on several occasions during dinner that Lady Brenda appeared quite enthralled with Lord Tabard. Why, it was beyond him. He was a potbellied middle-aged man in possession of an ill temper when he did not get his way. But if Dante could be assured Lady Brenda's affections were elsewhere engaged, that was one less female his grandmother could foist upon him, and he could turn his attention to more important matters.

Lady Brenda accepted his arm, but her attention was engaged elsewhere. Dante followed the direction of her gaze. It led straight to the boisterous Lord Tabard.

"I see that Lord Tabard is enjoying himself this evening."

"Oh? I hadn't noticed." The lady claimed nonchalance, but her inquisitive stare and subsequent question declared otherwise. "I've heard that Lord Tabard's estate is one of the finest in the county, and that he recently renovated the entire house. I've heard that Lord Tabard has offered to host a picnic. Is that true?"

"Yes, I believe so. Lord Tabard is also to host a ball in London."

"Oh yes, Lady Huntingdon did make a mention of that trivial detail. It is to be scheduled upon completion of the renovation, I believe." She glanced away as if she had given too much of her feelings away.

It dawned on Dante that Lady Brenda was not at all interested in Lord Tabard, but his estates and vast wealth. Playing devil's advocate, Dante inserted, "I believe he is making things ready for a new bride."

Lady Brenda stopped short, her hand squeezing Dante's arm with much more force than he thought possible from a woman of her petite stature. "He is engaged?"

Dante's assumptions were correct. "Not yet." The pressure from her hand eased with those two simple words. "I believe he is the market for his next viscountess." Lord Tabard's first wife had died leaving him without an heir, or any children for that matter. He had made it known that a wife who fulfilled his fondest desire of providing him with an heir would have whatever she desired.

"And has he discovered said lady?"

Clearly Lady Brenda was willing to trade love, good companionship, and looks for money. Not that Dante thought very highly of Lady Brenda to begin with, but the woman went down several notches in his esteem.

"Not that I'm aware."

Lady Brenda's features lightened as she sighed, clearly relieved that she had not lost her opportunity. "If you will excuse me, I believe I will rejoin my friends."

Any normal man might be offended by her request, but Dante wanted to be rid of her just as much as she apparently wanted to be rid of him.

"Not at all." No sooner had the words exited his mouth than Lady Brenda sauntered away in the direction of Lord Tabard. He did not wish the woman ill, but by pursuing a life with Lord Tabard, she was sentencing herself to a miserable existence, of that much he was certain.

Relieved that he no longer had to worry about any advancements from Lady Brenda, Dante searched the room. He needed to solve the next conundrum.

Mrs. Weston and Miss Albryght were off to themselves in a quiet corner of the room. He knew exactly what his next course of action would be. Ignoring the daggers his grandmother shot at him, he strolled toward the two ladies he believed could aid him.

"Good evening, Mrs. Weston, Miss Albryght." They looked warily at each other. "Might I have a word with you—on the veranda in ten minutes." It wasn't a question or even a demand; it was a request, and he did not give them any time to refuse. After speaking his desire, he turned and took his leave of them. Out of the corner of his eye, he saw the approval in his grandmother's eyes. Clearly she had not heard any of his transaction otherwise. Dante was most certain that she would interfere. It was best to keep up pretenses than to deal with his grandmother at this moment.

Dante circumnavigated the perimeter of the room before ducking out onto the veranda, hopefully unseen. He did not have to wait long for Mrs. Weston and Miss Albryght to join him.

"Thank you for meeting me. There is a matter of great importance that I must discuss with you." Dante kept his tone hushed, wanting to avoid those who might try to eavesdrop.

"You must be referring to Miss Quintin," Mrs. Weston said in a protective voice.

"Why would we give you any information that would…?"

"Isabel, please," Mrs. Weston put her hand on Miss Albryght's shoulder as she stepped in closer to Dante. "We need to hear what Lord Huntingdon has to say *before* we scold."

This was going to prove to be more difficult than he first assumed. What was he to expect? These were her closest friends. He would first have to earn their trust.

"Mrs. Weston, you have known me for quite some time. I don't believe that I have ever done anything to jeopardize that friendship."

"No, you have not." He could sense Mrs. Weston's resolve begin to soften toward him. "What is it that you desire of us?"

"I need to see her. Please tell me where she hides herself away during the day."

Although the words were hushed, they were anything but soft. "And why should we when you broke her heart?" Isabel stood her ground, waiting for him to answer.

"It was not as if I set out to break her heart. The day I went to ask for her hand, her father informed me that she had died. He had apprised everyone in the village of her demise and even held a small funeral for her. Why would I believe otherwise?" He fought to control the rage boiling inside. He ran a frustrated hand through his hair, and felt it tremble against his skull. "Don't you understand? I didn't know." The words came out on a jagged breath. He fought hard to tamp down the pain that had never gone away and had lain dormant for the past eight years, festering inside, eating away at him.

"What about the letters she sent? Why didn't you respond?" Miss Albryght's tone had softened, but her words still held a sharp edge about them.

"I never received her letters." Dante turned and clutched the cold balustrade, hoping for some relief from the boiling anger.

Mrs. Weston stepped in closer. "We will help you."

Chapter Eight

The blue sky sprinkled with fluffy clouds was a soothing balm to her problems. Anastasia knew she should not have ventured from the room for fear of seeing Lord Huntingdon or his grandmother, but many of the guests still had not risen, including most of the men. After the entertainments from last night, Philippa had said that she would be surprised if the women were on time to the scavenger hunt that was to take place later that afternoon.

Anastasia lay back on the crisp grass and gazed up into the clear blue sky. White puffy clouds danced across the great expanse, their shape taking form in her imagination.

The outline of a horse galloping in the meadow pranced across the sky. Another cloud shifted, revealing a heart. The wind carried the heart, dissolving it into the breeze and reminding her of her own broken heart.

It just didn't seem fair. Men were allowed all sorts of freedom. Men were forgiven for foolish youthful mistakes, where women were condemned for the rest of their lives for following their heart. Anastasia reflected on all that she had lost, how she had disgraced her family, lost the only man she ever had loved, and her only child.

She splayed her hand across her flat stomach, remembering the feel of her precious baby kicking inside. She had not known what the future would hold, but she had vowed to her unborn child that she would love her and care for her and never abandon her, the way her own family had abandoned Anastasia in her time of need.

Promises that she was not able to keep. She was not able to protect her child from death.

On a stormy, horrible night, her daughter had been born. She was so tiny and fragile. In her short life, she never complained or cried. It was the most precious gift Anastasia had ever been given and for a brief time her world was bright against the dark and gloomy unknown. But her joy had been short-lived. With the rising sun came her daughter's last breath.

The hard lump that had lived in her chest resurfaced with full force. Anastasia remembered the grief and pain of losing her baby as if it were only yesterday. She had held her tiny daughter as she took her last breath. Had held her for hours afterward, hoping, praying that she would breathe again, that her precious little life would be restored. But it never happened.

Tears streamed down Anastasia's cheeks, soaked up by the hair at her temples. She turned onto her side, burying her face into her arm, giving into the grief that still tormented her.

* * *

Over the past years, Dante had often imagined seeing her, wished that she had not died. It would appear that his wish had come true.

He kept glancing at the clock. Dante could have sworn that it was later than it actually was. It seemed as if time was standing still—or worse, moving backwards. He paced the length of the room, picked up a book to read, and then just as quickly putting it down before he made another pass about the room.

The clock on the mantel must be broken. It still wasn't time. Patience was not something he currently possessed. He went to his desk and pulled a clean sheet of paper from the top drawer. He massaged the pencil in his hand and then began to sketch an oval. Almond-shaped eyes peered back through long eyelashes framed by delicate brows. He quickly added a dainty nose. As if by its own volition, his hand began to sketch the outline of full plump lips. Long waves of hair cascaded about her shoulders, disappearing into faded lines.

He leaned back in his chair and gazed at his creation. Remembrances of her waltzing with him the other night flooded his memory. She had not changed one bit.

At long last, the clock began to chime. It was time.

Careful not to be seen by any early risers, Dante slinked through the house like a common thief. Once outside, he skirted the perimeter of the manor, careful to stay clear of windows that could alert the occupants to his flight.

With his destination clear in his mind, he picked up his pace and followed the path that led to the meadow. He would not stop to enjoy the wild violet orchids, or gaze up into the branches wondering what bird he might spy. There were more important things to discover.

Slowing his pace to catch his breath, Dante walked down the slight slope. In the near distance he spotted her, lying on the grass, crying. The wound in his heart from losing her the first time cracked a little more. He did not like to see her upset. He never wanted to see her hurt.

The bright sunlight peeked out from behind a large cloud and blurred his vision. Doubt crept in and he wondered whether she was flesh and blood or an aberration, a figment of his imagination. Visions such as these had often haunted him through the years.

He approached with a mixture of caution and curiosity. He knew her to be real, but he worried that she would disappear just the same. As he neared, her sobs broke through the calm summer day. The green blades of grass swayed in the gentle breeze. A hawk let out a cry, matching Anna's sorrowful weep. Abruptly, she sat up and smoothed the long auburn locks that had come loose and now blew against the wind. She took his breath away; she was even more beautiful than he remembered.

She stood, brushed off her skirt, and turned. The moment their eyes met, he knew she was not a vision, but flesh and blood. His first instinct was to pull her into his embrace, but common sense won out.

"Good Afternoon, Anastasia." He would not use her nickname—not yet anyway. She stilled, apparently too shocked to say anything. "Care to tell me why you are here at Paradiso?"

"I accompanied Miss Albryght to the house party," she whispered.

"You accompanied her?" He did not want to believe her. He wanted her to say that she came here to see him.

"Yes. I am her companion." Last night, Mrs. Weston had revealed the same information, but he had yet to learn why she was Miss Albryght's companion.

All these years she had been so close, and yet he believed her dead. Rage tore through his insides. Had Anna only pretended to be dead, to work as a lady's companion because she had not cared for him in the same way he had for her?

His imagination was destroying common sense. Why would she engineer such an elaborate scheme? He stepped in closer, searching her jade-green eyes for some clue as to how she felt, but all he saw were eyes that were swollen and puffy from crying. The color had drained from her features. She looked exhausted, but she still had that same sweetness that he found so endearing.

"You don't have to worry. As soon as this house party is over, I will be leaving." He could hear the sorrow and heartache intertwined in her words.

A horse whinnied from beyond the meadow. Dante turned to see who might be approaching. When he turned back around, Anna had already started to run toward the copse. Wasting no time, he followed her.

* * *

"Stop running away from me." Lord Huntingdon grabbed her arm and pulled her toward him. Eau de Cologne brought memories from the past to the fore. His voice softened. "Talk to me."

Anastasia stood still, feeling the warmth of his hand on her arm. She so desperately wanted to tell him—and yell at him, scream at him, and demand answers. Didn't he comprehend what she had endured because of his refusal? He didn't even refuse. He simply did not respond and left her all alone.

She pulled her arm free and took several steps back. She needed distance and begged her body not to react. She did not want to give into all the emotions colliding within her heart.

"No. You have no right to request anything of me." She took another step backward. Her body craved his nearness, but her mind needed the distance. He would not fool her again. One broken heart in a lifetime was enough for her. He had shattered her fairy tale into a thousand pieces. He left her without so much as a simple goodbye.

"Why did you not write to me?" She tried to keep the hurt from her voice, but she could not help it. The painful lump rose with each word she choked out.

Confusion streaked across his face. What lies would he concoct to ease his own conscience? Squaring her shoulders, she prepared herself for battle.

"You left me. You said you would write to me and you didn't." He began to shake his head as he took a step forward. She put up her hand to halt his movements. "And when I needed you most, you deserted me."

"I never received any of your letters. I don't know why, but I didn't." This time when he took a step, she did not stop him. "I never deserted you," his voice was deep, caring. Oh lord, how would she ever get through this?

Anastasia saw the sincerity in his eyes. She didn't know what to believe anymore. "But why did you not come to me?"

"I did, at the beginning of summer, just as I said I would." His features turned dark, lost in some painful memory. "Your father said you had died two weeks before in a carriage accident."

Searching the recesses of her mind, Anastasia tried to recall the date when her father had sent her away. "Oh lord," she whispered as the breath left her body. Her legs weakened beneath her.

Lord Huntingdon was at her side, holding her upright. "Anna?" he questioned, using the nickname he had given her.

He didn't know. She pressed her fingers to her temple. She could not think straight. Her world was spinning out of control. Every truth that she had clung to over the past eight years had been wrong.

"Anna, please talk to me."

"No," she said as she back away from him. "I can't... I need..." She could not bear the pain or the confusion. "I'm sorry."

Anastasia hurried away with all due haste. She kept running as fast as she could, past inquisitive servants and startled guests. The world around her was a sea of confusion and she was a tiny boat caught in a squall. She did not stop running until she entered her room and slammed the door closed.

Her head fell against the wood door with a thud. "Why?" she cried, the tears streaming down her face in torrents. "What crime have I committed to be punished so?"

The door she had been leaning on lurched forward as if someone was trying to enter. A knock sounded on the other side, close to her ear followed by Isabel's voice.

"Anastasia?"

Quickly she wiped the tears away but knew very well that her friends would see that she had been crying. At the least, she could possibly hide how much she had been crying. Pushing off the door, she took in a long shaky breath, and then reached for the knob.

The door opened and closed so fast that if Anastasia had not noticed Isabel and Philippa in the room, she would have thought she imagined the whole scene.

"What happened? Everyone is talking about how you stormed through the house knocking guests over and creating such a ruckus."

"It was not as bad as all that, Isabel," Philippa corrected Isabel and then turned her attention to Anastasia. "You saw Lord Huntingdon?"

Anastasia could not find the words, too afraid that the tears would start anew. She nodded her head, confirming Philippa's assumptions.

"Oh you poor thing." Philippa brought her into a snug embrace. "I'm sorry," she whispered into Anastasia's ear. "It is all my fault. I told him where you would be this morning."

Anastasia backed away. "Is that why you both insisted I go for a long morning walk?" She didn't need to look at their faces to know that Isabel and Philippa were both guilty. "Why?" That seemed to be a question that Anastasia was asking a lot as of late.

It was Philippa who spoke first, accepting most of the blame. "After dinner last night, Lord Huntingdon pleaded for our assistance."

"What did he say to you?" Anastasia didn't think he was lying to her earlier, but she was curious what he said to her friends just the same.

"He said that he never received any of the letters you sent." Philippa seemed uncomfortable with the direction that the conversation was turning.

Isabel continued where Philippa left off. "He said that your father told everyone that you died."

Tears started anew. Anastasia detested that after all these years her family could still generate such unwanted emotions from her.

"Why would they say such things?"

Anastasia could not answer Philippa's question without the hot tears streaming down her face. "My mother died in childbirth and my father always blamed me. Even my brothers had shared that anger. Perhaps it was a way to end his grief." Anastasia rubbed the back of her neck where the pain and stress had settled as her shoulders lurched with violent sobs.

"I don't believe Lord Huntingdon is as guilty as you think him to be, if at all, Anastasia." Isabel's practical voice broke through her sobs.

Sniffling back the tears, Anastasia murmured, "As much as I cannot believe I am saying this, I agree, Isabel. I just don't know what to do."

Philippa rubbed Anastasia's arm. "Join us for the scavenger hunt."

Anastasia looked at Philippa as if she were mad.

Chapter Nine

"Are you sure you're confident with the plan?" Dante was too nervous for words. He would have preferred more time to plan, but time was not on his side.

The moment he had seen his grandmother's list for the scavenger hunt, an idea had sprung to mind, but he needed help executing the plan. That is where Mrs. Weston came in. He was prepared to plead his case to her when Mrs. Weston had entered the library stating that she believed his intentions toward Anastasia to be sincere and would do whatever it took to bring them together.

"For the umpteenth time, yes. Isabel and I are prepared to do whatever is necessary. I have already given Lord Colt his instructions as well."

"I just don't want anything to go wrong." It was fortuitous that Dante was even able to catch a glimpse of the list beforehand. He didn't want to take any chances.

"It won't, trust me," Mrs. Weston assured.

Dante wished he shared Mrs. Weston's confidence. The last thing he wanted was to lose Anna again. He wanted to make amends for the past and build a future with her. There was no doubt in his mind that they were meant to be together. Eight years did not wash away the love they had shared—no, still shared. And then there was his grandmother's ultimatum. He was not going to take any chances where Grandmother was concerned. First he would settle the past and ensure his future with Anastasia, and then he would deal with his grandmother.

"Do you really believe that Anastasia will forgive me?" Even to his own ears, he sounded like an unseasoned schoolboy.

Mrs. Weston smiled brightly at him. "Yes, I do. It isn't so much that she has to forgive as much as she has to let go of the past. There are still many unanswered questions. It may take time, but I know how much she cares for you."

Dante ran a frustrated hand through his hair. "I still don't understand why her family felt the need to tell me she was dead, or why I never received any of her letters." For one brief moment he thought his grandmother might have been behind it all, but he had not mentioned his intentions to his grandparents until the day before he left for Plymouth. By that point in time, rumors of Anastasia's death had already been circulating round her village.

"I know, but with all my heart I hope that after today, both of you will be able to put the past to rest." Her reassuring smile eased some of his tension. "Now," Mrs. Weston began with a clap of her hands, "after your grandmother calls out the groups, Isabel will guide Lord Tabard to the obelisk. Are you certain that Lady Brenda has her cap set on Lord Tabard?"

"Yes."

It was an odd pairing, but only just that morning Lady Brenda informed Dante that her affections were engaged elsewhere. He was certain that the prospect of being a viscountess with unlimited funds at her disposal was much more thrilling than being a countess, despite Lord Tabard's habits and temper.

"Excellent. Anastasia and I will go straight to the grotto."

"What do you intend to do with Mr. Bacon? He is likely not to want to leave Anastasia's side." Dante had suspected that the man was smitten with Anna, and Dante intended to put an end to that once and for all.

"I will tell him that I am unable to walk for any distance and that Miss Quintin will keep me company while he sees to the first clue. If I hint that Anastasia would like to win, I suspect Mr. Bacon would find a way to the moon and back if it meant pleasing her."

"You suspect him enamored of Anastasia as well?"

"Of course. A man does not boast every accomplishment and fawn all over a woman every chance he gets if he has no interest in her. Especially when the woman has shown no interest in him whatsoever."

Mrs. Weston's declaration of Anna's lack of interest eased the jealousy that was coiling inside. She began to turn and walk away when Dante stopped her. "I know that the circumstances are odd at best, but I appreciate what you are doing. Thank you."

"You do not need to thank me. Just make her happy."

* * *

Anastasia didn't know what it was about Paradiso, if it was being this close to *him* or having to face the past, but being here brought out all sorts of emotions that she had thought she buried.

She was so tired. Tired of hiding her problems and feelings. Tired of wanting things she couldn't have. For the rest of today she was not going to be that person. Included in what she wouldn't do, she would not think about her encounter with Lord Huntingdon earlier that morning. She was going to enjoy the day and think about…well, tomorrow.

The sun shone bright in the blue sky. A cool breeze caressed the landscape. The sound of water lapping against the bridge added to the symphony of nature's sounds. Anastasia breathed in the fresh country air. For the first time in eight years, she felt alive, and believed that the future held some possibilities for her. Perhaps she was finding peace at last.

Everyone had gathered on the veranda, awaiting the instructions for the day's event. Isabel had overheard Lady Brenda tell Miss Saunders that there was to be a scavenger hunt. Anastasia had never participated in one but was intrigued with the idea of such a diversion.

"Ladies and gentlemen, please gather round," Gibbs instructed the guests. "Her ladyship will detail the rules."

Gibbs stepped aside, allowing the formidable Lady Huntingdon to take center stage.

"Each group will have a list of ten items that must be found. The first group who finds all ten items wins the scavenger hunt. I must warn you, the items could be located anywhere. There is a clue on each page to start you on the correct path."

There were giggles and sideways glances passing about. Anastasia could not help but wonder what sort of mischief the other guests were going to discover in addition to their items.

All the young ladies gathered around Lady Huntingdon in anticipation. Anastasia presumed that Lord Huntingdon was the partner of choice for those giggling damsels. She did not care who he was partnered with, she told herself.

Lady Huntingdon's voice broke through the chatter. "I have here a list of the teams, which were randomly selected."

Anastasia doubted that very much. If she had learned anything over the course of the past several days, it was that Lady Huntingdon never left anything to chance. She listened as Lady Huntingdon read the teams aloud.

"Lord Tabard, you are paired with Miss Albryght. Lord Huntingdon, you will be paired with Lady Brenda." With that announcement, the sound of disappointment resounded amongst the ladies. "Mrs. Weston, you are paired with Mr. Bacon." She continued to read the groups.

Ten minutes later, Anastasia was the only one who had not been called. Lady Huntingdon turned to address Anastasia.

"Miss Quintin, since I was not expecting you to participate," the disdain in Lady Huntingdon's voice was clear, "you may assist Mrs. Weston and Mr. Bacon." Of course she was paired with Mr. Bacon. The man had all but proposed to her over dinner. He simply could not fathom that she was not interested in him.

Out of the corner of her eye, Anastasia saw Lord Huntingdon glance over at her. She would not give him the satisfaction of responding to his scheming grandmother. It was clear that Lady Huntingdon did not want her anywhere near her grandson.

Anastasia did not respond, but simply forced a smile and joined her friends. At least, it was considerate to pair her with someone she knew. She assumed it had more to do with the fact that Lady Huntingdon did not want Anastasia to mingle with her more socially superior guests. Whatever the reason, she was thankful. Distance from Lord Huntingdon and all that she had learnt would give her a reprieve from her cascading emotions.

Anastasia did not pay attention to Lady Huntingdon's further ramblings. She looked down at the sheet that Philippa held in her hand, trying to determine where the first item might be.

Philippa tugged at her hand. "Don't say anything; just play along," she whispered before turning her attention to Mr. Bacon. "Are you ready, Mr. Bacon?" Philippa said as she hobbled away from the main group and toward a cropping of trees.

Anastasia was about to ask Philippa why she was limping when she squeezed Anastasia's hand with great force. Their eyes met, and Philippa shook her head, pleading Anastasia to be silent. *What was Philippa up to?*

When they were concealed from the others, Philippa turned her attention to Mr. Bacon. "I don't believe I am feeling up to traversing all over in search of the items. Perhaps you wouldn't mind finding the first few items on your own?" Philippa smiled brightly, charming Mr. Bacon. "Miss Quintin and I will be eternally grateful."

"Of course not, Mrs. Weston. I will see our team to victory." One would have thought he was going off to fight in a war rather than just participate in a scavenger hunt. He turned and disappeared down the path.

"What…?" Philippa shook her head, begging Anastasia to keep silent. Chirping birds and rustling leaves were all that could be heard. After several more agonizing seconds passed, Anastasia tugged on Philippa's sleeve and mouthed, "What is going on?"

Grabbing Anastasia's hand, Philippa whispered with great excitement, "Let's go."

Philippa did not give Anastasia the chance to respond, but pulled her toward the direction of the footbridge. Hiding behind some trees, Philippa glanced this way and that.

"What are you doing?" Anastasia wondered once again if her friend had gone mad. Philippa was a free spirit and a little impulsive at times, but she was acting…well, just plain odd.

"Shh," Philippa murmured under her breath. "You never know who is lurking about."

And with that final statement, she pulled Anastasia's hand, practically dragging her across the bridge until they were on the other side and once again hidden by trees.

Philippa leaned against an obliging tree, her hand clasped against her chest as it rose up and down with heavy breaths. She giggled into the wind. "I don't believe anyone spied us."

"Will you please tell me what you are up to?" Anastasia knew she sounded more like a worried governess to a young child than a full-grown woman, but she had wanted to enjoy the scavenger hunt, not play whatever game Philippa had decided on.

"Not yet," was all that she said before she grabbed Anastasia's hand yet again and walked off at a brisk pace, dragging her behind. The earth rose steadily as they meandered on the path. She really should protest, but Philippa's infectious excitement combined with curiosity was starting to get the better of Anastasia. And besides, she trusted Philippa. She would never bring trouble down upon Anastasia.

The path started to narrow and formed a small valley. The sweet scent of damp earth tickled her nostrils. She looked up and saw a large spider web shimmering in the sunlight. The branches overhead formed a canopy of sorts, shading them from the afternoon sun. She felt like she was wrapped in a green velvety cocoon. Anastasia was thankful for the silence. She enjoyed seeing nature in all its splendid glory.

When they came to a bend in the path, Philippa began to guide Anastasia through the overgrowth. The earth on the one side formed a mossy hill easily ten feet tall. But their way appeared to be blocked by a large shrub.

"This way," Philippa said as she disappeared behind the bush.

Anastasia followed wondering what they were going to find. She pushed her way through and saw Philippa standing at a recessed door framed by earth.

"What are we doing here?"

"There is something inside that I want you to see." The smile on Philippa's face was full of mischief. Everyone was searching for their scavenger hunt items and instead, they were trekking through the brush on some wild adventure. Philippa pushed the door open and stood to one side.

"Aren't you going in?"

Philippa shook her head. "Someone has to stand guard. Now, hurry up." She opened the door a couple of feet. A cool breeze whooshed past them.

The whole situation was highly suspicious. Anastasia crossed her arms and in a firm tone said, "Not until you tell me what is going on."

Philippa sucked in a deep breath. "Nothing. I just want you to see the view from inside the grotto. The path bends a little to the right, if you follow the light, and it will take you to the statue of Venus."

Anastasia gave Philippa one of her skeptical looks. She did not know what Philippa was up to. Surely Lady Huntingdon would come along and discover they had not been participating in the scavenger hunt, leaving the unfortunate Mr. Bacon a lonely participant. As much as she did not care for him, she did feel guilty about abandoning him, and then there was Lady Huntingdon. Anastasia doubted that even Philippa was strong enough to endure that sort of lecture.

They stood staring at each other for countless seconds, casting the other incredulous looks. If Isabel were here, she would have burst out in laughter at their ridiculous facial expressions. It really was a battle of sorts to see who would give in first.

"Fine." Anastasia's arms fell to her side in defeat. Under normal circumstances, she would have resisted far longer, but there had been nothing normal about their stay thus far; why break the pattern? "I don't know what this all about, but I will indulge you just this once." They both knew good and well that it wouldn't be just this once. Philippa seemed to bring out that more free-spirit side to Anastasia that had been dormant, but certainly not dead. Even Isabel had become more playful under Philippa's tutelage. She really had been good for everyone that resided at Knights Hall.

"You won't regret this." Philippa gave her a quick kiss on her cheek before nudging her inside. It took several seconds for her eyes to adjust to the darkened space. She closed her eyes, counted to five, and then slowly opened them again. In the distance, a shaft of light caressed the stone walls, creating intricate patterns that Anastasia found most intriguing.

A cool wind encircled her, causing a shiver. Her arms prickled with goose bumps, and Anastasia rubbed her arms with fervor as she drifted toward the light. Water trickled down the walls and streamed along its base. The narrow stone hall opened onto a circular chamber. At the far end was a wide opening that overlooked Paradiso's lake. Through the opening she saw the footbridge that she and Philippa had crossed only a short time ago.

The sun shimmered on the lake, casting shades of white and gold. The wind rippled the waters creating an elaborate dance. "How beautiful," she whispered into the tranquil stillness.

"I was hoping you would like the view."

Anastasia turned at the sound of Lord Huntingdon's voice. The air caught in her throat. Despite the coolness of the underground chamber, she felt suddenly warm all the way down to her toes. This was not good. How was she to maintain her nonchalant attitude with him standing so near? She didn't want to be affected.

"Please don't."

"Anna, please talk to me. What happened? Why won't you just talk to me?"

He stood so close to her. She could feel him, feel his strength as it wrapped her in a protective cocoon. She had been drawn to it before. But too much time had passed, and too much heartache.

"I can't," she whispered out as she tried to move past him, but he grabbed her hand. That tingling sensation that she had spent years trying to forget threatened to overtake her countenance. How was that possible with just one touch?

"I am not going to lose you again," his voice was barely a whisper against her face. She could hear the pain, but she could not bring herself to look at him. "Don't you understand? I can't lose you again."

Anastasia knew if she turned around and looked into his eyes that she would not be able to resist him. She was so torn. She desperately wanted to believe that they could have a future, that he had been telling the truth. Could what happened all those years ago be just a terrible misunderstanding?

"I...just don't know if... That was a long time ago," she managed to say through heavy breaths. "I don't know who you are." He was an earl now. She was nothing more than a companion to Miss Albryght. Their stations were vastly different.

His fingers caressed her hand, but he maintained his distance. "I am still the same man I was eight years ago. I don't understand what happened, or why I never received your letters, or why your family told me that you were dead." He took a cautious step closer. "But I will be damned if I lose you again. I love you. I always have."

Why did he have to say those words that made her question all her beliefs?

"Lord Huntingdon, I..."

"Why won't you call me Dante?"

"That would suggest a certain intimacy that—" She swallowed the hard lump that was threatening what little self-control she had left. She pulled her hand from his and took several steps back, colliding with the damp rock wall.

He closed some of the distance she had just tried to create. "We have been intimate." His words rushed her senses. "We don't have to be strangers anymore."

Anastasia shook her head. "It won't work. Too mu–much has happened," she gasped out between sobs. She detested that she allowed herself to cry in front of him, but she couldn't stop. Too much anger and hurt had been simmering over the years and she wasn't prepared to let it go that easily. "I..." Her head started to pound as past betrayals rushed through her mind. She ducked under his arm and tried to scurry away from him, but he caught her hand and swung her into him.

"Stop running away from me," was all he said as he took her mouth in a soft yet demanding kiss.

The moment their lips touched it was as if no time had passed. Time rewound and sweet exploration began. She was lost in that kiss. He slanted his mouth and claimed her, branded her his own. Instinctively her hands roamed up his chest, settling at the base of his neck.

"Please say I haven't lost you," he whispered as he broke the kiss, nuzzling into her neck. "I cannot bear to lose you again. Do you have any notion how I suffered when I learned of your de..."

She was thankful that he did not say that word again. It was odd to be referred to in that state of eternal demise and she did not like it.

As if hearing her thoughts and wishing for her to feel she was alive, his lips renewed their exploration, soft, needing kisses that demanded her attention. She thought she would die from the sheer pleasure of being held by him. Strong arms kept her firmly in place. She did not want this moment to end. It had been so long since she felt like this. Everything she had feared that had been washed away, all her hopes and dreams from the past began to resurface.

"Please say I haven't lost you." He kept repeating as he streamed kisses down the column of her neck. The tingling kept her from thinking straight.

"Dante...I..."

"You said my name," he smiled against her lips. She could feel the energy and desire course through him. He cupped her cheek and looked into her eyes. "Say it again."

"Dante, I...I missed you so much." Anastasia could not fight the tears, and part of her did not want to. She looked into his soft brown eyes and saw the pain and longing that matched her own. She still did not know if past hurts could be healed so quickly, but every fiber of her being wanted to believe that they *could* build a life together.

As if suspecting where her thoughts had turned, Dante said, "I am not asking for you to forget what happened, or to pretend that it never happened. I am asking for forgiveness. I am asking for you to let me in, to share your life." He brought his forehead down to hers. He inhaled deeply and on an exhale said, "Please tell me that I am not too late."

Butterflies battered her stomach. Dante was so close, clouding her thoughts. Her mind wanted answers, but in the end Anastasia let her heart speak for her. "You are not too late."

No sooner had the words left her mouth, then the sound of Philippa calling into the chamber reached her ears. "Someone is coming."

"I have to go." Anastasia started to retreat when Dante pulled her in for another kiss. Her pulse quickened with each gentle stroke of his tongue.

Dante pulled back and let out a slight sigh. "I suppose I must let you go."

"Yes, I do not think it wise to get caught." She wanted to add especially by his grandmother. Truth be told, the woman terrified her.

Philippa had begun to call out her name with great urgency. Anastasia gave him a quick kiss on the cheek and then raced back toward the entrance.

"Come on," Philippa said as she pulled Anastasia through the opening and closed the door behind her.

The two rushed away in silence. It was only once they crossed over the footbridge did Philippa speak. "Judging by the smile on your face, I suspect that you enjoyed the view?"

"Very much so." Anastasia was positively giddy. Although there was one confession hanging over her head, she would not let it diminish her current joy. Somehow the bright day paled in comparison to the brightness Dante had ignited inside of her.

"I see you are recovered, Mrs. Weston." Lady Huntingdon's stern voice brought them both to an immediate halt.

Anastasia kept silent. The joy she had been experiencing had been quashed under Lady Huntingdon's rude tone. Philippa was far more experienced in dealing with arrogant ladies of the *ton*.

"Yes, I am. Thank you for inquiring, Lady Huntingdon. These things do happen from time to time."

Philippa's blasé tone did not sit well with Lady Huntingdon. "I expect there to be no more shenanigans from either of you. Mr. Bacon has done a splendid job tackling the list on his own." She turned her attention to Anastasia. "He was inquiring after you, Miss Quintin and I took the liberty in telling him that you would welcome his attention. In fact, he has requested a special audience with you before the ball day after tomorrow."

Anastasia was fuming. How was she to avoid Mr. Bacon for two days? The audacity of this woman. Who was she to make such bold assumptions? *Dante's grandmother*, the cautious, reasonable voice in her head reminded. No matter how much they loved each other, Lady Huntingdon would always try and come between them. Well, she would not give Lady Huntingdon the satisfaction of controlling her life, and she would begin with this evening. Anastasia would claim a headache and retreat for the remainder of the day.

Clearly pleased with herself, Lady Huntingdon ended with a sly smile. "Until this evening."

Both Anastasia and Philippa mumbled their farewells under their breath.

"That was a disaster," Philippa uttered. "Now, you must tell me everything."

⚮ ⚮ ⚮

Pacing the cool interior of the grotto, Dante waited for his opportunity to leave undetected. Through the opening, across the lake, he had spotted his grandmother storming across the footbridge. He was not prepared to deal with her at that moment. He did not want anything to dampen his mood.

Even after holding her, kissing her, breathing in her scent, Dante could not believe that his Anna was alive. All the years of heartache were washed away the moment she had said his name. It was the sweetest sound in the world.

There was much preparation before the ball. His grandmother would be furious, but he did not care. This was his chance at love and he was going to take it.

Chapter Ten

Anastasia was a bundle of nerves. Excitement had collided with nervousness, creating an emotion too powerful to name. She desperately wanted to believe that her fairy tale would have a happy ending. She had not felt this way in such a long time, not since that first day at the cottage.

Isabel had made excuses for Anastasia, claiming she was indisposed with another headache; she only hoped that no one would suspect contrary. Strolling along the path that led to the obelisk, she was surrounded by a woodland area.

Everything seemed more vibrant, more alive. Fresh pine mingled with the faint scent of orchids. The chirp of the birds even seemed louder, happier. Anastasia twirled down the path, lost in the loveliness around her. She could not control the joy that spilled over from her heart and coursed through the rest of her body.

Laughter halted her dance.

"And what do you find so amusing?" She questioned Dante who was leaning against a tree, looking entirely too handsome.

"You." He pushed off the tree and picked up a basket and began to approach her. "You can't imagine how many times I have dreamt of you like that."

She raised a brow. "Twirling about like a child?"

"There is nothing childlike about you." Anastasia could feel the heat flush her cheeks as Dante's eyes roamed over her ankles to lips and back again. Her heart skipped a beat, but she remained still. For a brief moment, she thought he was going to kiss her. Instead, he extended his arm. "Shall we?"

"Where are we going?"

"Since we are missing the impromptu picnic being hosted by Lord Tabard, I thought we could have one of our own."

"I'm rather glad to miss seeing him. He is quite disagreeable."

Dante laughed. "That is a mild way to put it."

"I don't want to talk of disagreeable things. Not today at least." Anastasia was still not ready to discuss what happened. She didn't want to keep secrets, but she hoped that Dante would give her a little more time. It was a delicate matter and her heart remained a fragile thing.

"What would you like to talk about?"

* * *

The space between her brows crinkled and Anna had kept silent for the longest time. They had just emerged from the wooded trail when she finally answered. "Clouds," she giggled with delight.

Clouds? He was just about to question her choice of topic when he remembered her fondness for discovering images hidden in the clouds. "Then you are in luck, my lady." He opened the basket and pulled out a small blanket. "I have just the accessory to fulfill your desire."

Anna took the blanket from him and whipped it open. The white rectangle floated to the earth like snow on a blustery day. Dante set the basket down at one end and before he could offer assistance Anna had already sat down and was staring up at the clouds.

"I see a castle in the sky with great big moat."

Dante sat down next her, the scent of lavender and honey teasing him to edge closer. He looked up. "A moat no less? Is that to keep marauding barbarians at bay?" He glimpsed at her out of the corner of his eye. In some ways, it was as if not a day had passed. She remained as lovely as ever, and his feelings had never faltered. He remembered fondly their first picnic. They had played this game back then too.

"What are you thinking?" Anna had brought her knees up and was resting her cheek on them.

"I was thinking of our first picnic."

She began to laugh. "It didn't end well." He must have cast a puzzled look. She began to explain, "Don't you remember? It had begun to rain and when we ran for cover, I lost my slipper, and then you tore your jacket."

He had forgotten about the rain. "Despite your lost slipper and the jacket I had never cared for in the first place, it was a perfect day."

"I agree." She took in a jagged breath and turned away, but not before he saw the sadness and hurt that lingered in her eyes.

"Won't you tell me…?"

"I do not want to discuss any unpleasantness today." She stood as she said the words and then ran off toward the obelisk.

Dante didn't know anything that she had been through for the past eight years, but something told him that he would not like the answer. He was not going to upset her with talk of their time apart; he just wanted to spend what little time remained of their afternoon together talking and reminiscing.

* * *

Dante did not know how he was going to make it through the evening without trying to kiss Anastasia. She looked positively edible in her pale blue gown. He wasn't the only one who appeared to notice as well.

Mr. Bacon had entered the room and dashed straight for her. Dante was fuming, but with his grandmother present, he knew better than to try and intervene. Grandmother was still reeling over his disappearance earlier in the day. Her punishment came in the none-too-subtle hints about what an excellent wife Lady Brenda would make. *Right. For Lord Tabard.*

Dante saw Anna's forced smile and refused to let her deal with the likes of Mr. Bacon any longer. With a casual gait that he did not feel, Dante went to her side.

"Good evening, Miss Quintin." He nodded his head toward her. The second their eyes met, a delicious blush stained her cheeks. He turned his attention to the obnoxious gentleman who had only moments ago discomposed the woman Dante loved. "Mr. Bacon. How are you this evening?"

The man cleared his voice, obviously uncomfortable in Dante's presence. "Fine, yes, quite… Excellent house party, Lord Huntingdon." He fumbled through a series of incoherent words.

"I was just speaking to Miss James." Dante leaned in, lowering his voice so as not to be overheard. "She was inquiring after you."

Mr. Bacon's eyes brightened with interest. "You don't say? Well," he puffed out his large chest, "I believe I will search her out." He bowed to Anna and then took his leave.

"Thank you for rescuing me, but I do not believe it was kind of you to subjugate poor Miss James to the dull conversation that she will surely have to endure."

"Ah, that is where you are wrong." Although Anna eyed him with curiosity, he did not respond right away, not until she gave him that sideways smile that he had always loved. "I have it on good authority that Miss James is indeed smitten with Mr. Bacon." Dante leaned in and whispered, "I believe it a mutual fondness for marzipan that brought them together."

Anna let out a giggle. "Marzipan?" She raised a delicate brow.

Dante chuckled at her query. "No, but I do know that she fancies him."

Anna shook her head, clearly not believing him.

"I've missed you." He whispered out the words so that no one might hear.

She lowered her lashes and offered a smile. "Me too."

"Will you meet…?"

"Durante, I need you." His grandmother's words broke through their interlude. She had stood and began to approach them, her hand extended in front of her, prepared to edge him along.

"Go on," Anna mouthed.

Dante bowed and reluctantly walked away, hoping that his grandmother did not suspect where his feelings lay. There was a time and place to confront his grandmother, and it was not now, in front of all their guests.

* * *

As Anastasia watched him walk away, a pang struck her heart. She had suspected that his grandmother did not approve of her presence and she did not know what she could do to earn her favor. Just as on previous nights, Anastasia was last to enter to the dining hall and seated farthest from Dante. The dinner passed just as it had on previous occasions with her hardly noticing the quality of the food or conversation that was being spoken around her.

After dinner, the ladies retreated to the Italian room while the men retired to the library. Anastasia did not want to be cornered by Lady Huntingdon again and made sure to stay close to Philippa and Isabel. But that did not stop the constant glares coming from Lady Huntingdon, which had increased, if that were at all possible. Anastasia took comfort in knowing that her two dearest friends were close at hand.

"It is a beautiful evening, and the moonlight is so bright; I believe I would like a walk in the garden." Isabel's loud statement startled the ladies that were sitting near to them, earning her scornful looks.

"I believe that I will join you as well," Philippa's voice was equally loud. What were they up to? "Anastasia, would you care to join us?"

She suspected that even if she did not want to, Philippa and Isabel would insist. She stood and followed her friends toward the French doors that led out into the garden. Anastasia noticed that Lady Huntingdon had followed with them with a stern gaze, but did not get up.

When they were a safe distance from the house, Anastasia questioned, "What are the two of you up to?"

"Shh." Philippa glanced over Anastasia's shoulder. "I don't believe anyone followed us," she muttered before tugging Anastasia's hand and pulling her toward the hedge maze. It did not take long to reach the maze, and once they entered, the house disappeared from sight.

"Thank you, Mrs. Weston and Miss Albryght." She heard Dante's deep voice before she saw him emerge from around the corner, his features still concealed by the shadows.

"You arranged this?" Anastasia did not ask the question to any one of them in particular.

"How else was I to spend a moment alone with you without all the curious onlookers?"

As if they sensed they were interrupting Anastasia and Dante, Philippa and Isabel began to back away.

"We will wait at the opening," Philippa said on a giggle. "Don't be too long."

The moment her friends disappeared into the shadows, Dante pulled Anastasia into his embrace and kissed her softly. Her toes curled in her satin shoes. Not even the night air could cool her inflamed desire.

"What happens when we are caught?" She asked breathless. It was a practical question, and, apparently, Dante had already thought of all the answers.

"We won't get caught. The men are in the library and not even my grandmother is bold enough to venture in there while the men are taking their cigars and brandy. And besides, Colt is covering for me on the off chance that my grandmother gets inquisitive."

He cupped her face, stroking her cheek with his ungloved hand. "I could not wait to see you any longer."

"It rather impossible to even have the briefest of conversations with Lady Huntingdon always glaring in my direction. I do not believe she cares for me."

"She does not care for anyone." There was no sadness in his voice. What had that cold, stern woman done to harden his heart? "I don't want to talk about my grandmother when I only have you alone for a few minutes."

"What do you wish to do?" The words were laced with want and desire. Anastasia could hardly believe what she said. She had never been so forward in her entire life.

"This." Dante wasted no time bringing her full against his hard frame and kissed her. His tongue probed and danced with hers. Anastasia wrapped her arms about his neck, trying to touch even more of him. His hand roamed her backside, exploring its way down. He cupped her bottom and squeezed. She felt the breath leave her body replaced with a desire that she had not ever felt before.

"Please, Dante…" she begged against his mouth. It had been so long since she had found pleasure; she did not want the moment to end.

Dante pulled back. Even in the dim moonlight she could see his gaze narrow. He shifted his head this way and that. "Someone is coming," he murmured into her ear.

Anastasia opened her mouth to speak, but then heard a faint whistle in the distance followed by a soft giggle. She did not think it was Lady Huntingdon; that woman was not capable of such a joyous act.

"Meet me tomorrow at the pantheon at noon." He offered a quick kiss and then released her before he disappeared into the maze. With all due haste, Anastasia quickly rejoined her friends.

Were she and Dante ever to have more than just a few stolen moments alone?

Chapter Eleven

He had been standing by the tree for what seemed like an eternity. It had been an eternity. Eight long years was an eternity, especially when he thought he would never see her again. She was late. Only by a few minutes, but nonetheless, she was late. He was hoping to spend more time with her today. Every moment they had had together thus far had been stolen away by duties, responsibilities, various activities, and his grandmother.

Everything had been planned down to the last detail. Once again, Dante would have never been able to get everything ready without Mrs. Weston and Miss Albryght's assistance. Dante paced around the columns on the portico. Patience was quickly becoming his Achilles heel. How long did it take for Miss Albryght to fetch Anastasia?

The pantheon was one of his favorite places on the estate and he could not wait to share it with Anna. The last time he tried to achieve this goal, it had ended in tragedy that he only overcame a few days ago when the woman he loved, donned in a green and blue mask, waltzed with him.

When would she arrive? His short nails scraped across the stone column with impatient angst. A disarming thought entered his mind. What if his grandmother had discovered his plans? No, he mustn't focus on the negative; that was all in the past now.

The sun shining through the branches momentarily blinded him. He closed his eyes, the light penetrating through his lids illuminating precious images from a long time ago of an auburn-haired beauty twirling in the early morning sunlight after a glorious night of declaring their love. He remembered each and every promise he had whispered that wondrous night. This was his chance to keep those promises.

Dante opened his eyes just as his Anna crested the hill with Miss Albryght loitering behind. He wanted to run out to Anna, take her in his arms and make love to her on the lush green grass. *Blast.* He needed to control his urges. The last thing either of them needed was to have his grandmother discover their clandestine affair. All would be revealed soon enough, but he wanted to cherish this moment before he informed his grandmother of his choice in bride.

Dante knew with certainty that his grandmother would throw a tantrum, but it was his life and he was going to start living it the way he saw fit.

Anna rushed into his arms and kissed him soundly on the lips. When she sighed, he took the opportunity to deepen the kiss. Their tongues tangled in a dance of seduction. Dante pulled her closer, wanting to feel every inch of her body against his.

A gust of wind whipped around them, bringing him back to his senses. They were outside where anyone might happen upon them. With great reluctance, he pulled back. Her lips were swollen, stained in a delicious shade of pink. Desire had deepened her jade eyes. He burned that impression of her into his mind. Later, in the quiet of his studio he would paint her just as she was now.

"Come, I have a surprise for you." He guided her to a secret entrance, hidden behind one of the wide columns. He pushed the heavy door open a couple of feet. "Follow me," he said, grasping her hand, pulling her through the dark passageway.

* * *

"I will follow you anywhere." *Just don't leave me again.* The unspoken words hovered in the air threatening to destroy the moment.

"I want you right beside me where I can see you, love you, embrace you." His words squashed any lingering fears.

As they passed through the dark corridor, she shrugged her shoulders with a shiver.

"Are you cold?" Dante said.

"A l-little," Anastasia replied with a chatter.

He stepped in and cupped her cheek. "Let me warm you." His words were uttered in a deep, seductive husk. Dante brushed a soft kiss across her lips. His tongue flicked her upper lip, begging her to open. She acquiesced with a sigh, giving him permission to plunder and take what had always been his.

The kiss slowed, and then softened to mere nibbles that were just as delectable. "At this rate, you will never see your surprise." His breath was jagged against her skin. He stroked his hand down the length of her arm. She shivered again, but not from the coolness of the space. She was still trying to regain her senses after that kiss they shared. Wrapping his other arm about her waist, he guided her further into the space.

Anastasia knew she needed to tell Dante exactly why her father had sent her away, but she did not want to ruin the moment. She had waited so long to be back in his arms. This time when the butterflies rose and fluttered, she did not wish them away. Instead she wanted to satisfy their urging.

Dante guided her several feet in the dim space before he stopped in front of a closed door. He leaned in and whispered into her ear, "Close your eyes."

Anastasia obeyed his request. She felt his breath on her eyelids, felt his lips brush along her cheek. "Oh, that feels…"

"It is just the beginning."

Anastasia did not want the moment to end. She felt him step away and then heard the door creak open. The fresh scent of lavender rushed her senses. "What are you…?"

"You will see in a moment. Just keep your eyes closed."

She could not keep from smiling. Anastasia did not know what he was about, but it warmed her insides to know that he had not changed in all these years. He remained caring and considerate, and still so charming.

She heard him shuffle about before he came beside her. Her body instinctively shifted toward him, wanting, desiring his closeness.

His hands caressed her shoulders. "Open your eyes, my lady," he whispered.

"Oh my," she said on a sigh.

Clearstory windows illuminated the crisp white marble space. A dozen marble statues lined the perimeter. The center aisle was strewn with lavender sprigs, creating a fragrant purple blanket. As Anastasia stepped further into the aromatic space, her body relaxed.

"What is all this? And…lavender." The words caught in her throat. "Oh, Dante…," she breathed out with a sigh.

Holding a single red rose, Dante came up beside her. "Do you not remember?" He trailed the red fragrant flower from her forehead down to her jaw. The sweet scent tickled her nose. She couldn't suppress the giggle that rose from a place she thought had died.

"How could I forget?" Her heartbeat quickened with the remembrance of their first time together. He had laid a blanket of flowers in the cottage. She turned into him, nuzzled against his chest. She heard his heartbeat in time with her own. Anastasia was lost to the sensations that he stirred. It was as if not a moment had passed.

Dante's hands roamed her backside, edging down and then settling on her hips as he kneeled down before her. He looked up at her. "I never want to be parted from you again. Marry me, my lady."

Anastasia was speechless. She had dreamt of a moment like this, with him, but there was still something she needed to tell him.

"Dante, I…" Tears started to stream down her face.

He stood and gathered her into his embrace. "Shh, my love. You don't have to answer." His words were laced with pain, but also understanding.

Anastasia did not want him to think that she did not want to marry him. "I do want to marry you, b—"

"You do?" The words were riddled with uncertainty. Oh lord, she did not want to hurt him. Perhaps now wasn't the time to discuss such tribulations.

"It is one of my fondest desires."

No sooner had the words exited her mouth than Dante's lips found hers. The kiss was slow, sensual. She could not let this go any further without telling him everything. But before she could gather her senses, Dante pulled back.

"I have something for you."

"You have already…" Dante reached into his pocket and pulled out the treasured necklace. "My mother's necklace," she murmured. Sadness and joy surged through her body. She would never know the mother who had given Anastasia life only to lose her own, but the joy in having a small piece of something her mother loved had been a soothing balm to a child in mourning. "You had it all this time?"

"It never left my person." Dante took the necklace from her. "Turn around." He brought his hands over her head. The cool gold chain rested against her warm flesh. "There," he said as he clasped the necklace.

Anastasia reached for the cameo. "Oh, Dante," the tears started anew. She was truly far too emotional to speak at this moment. "Thank you, this means…the world to me."

"You mean the world to me." Dante showered her with kisses. "I want to announce our engagement tonight."

"Tonight?" She saw the look of hurt scour his face and quickly added, "It is not that I don't want to marry you. It just seems rather sudden."

"I wanted to marry you eight years ago. Somehow I don't think this is sudden," Dante teased as he kissed the tip of her nose.

She had missed their playful banter. "I suppose it's not," she acquiesced and then offered her lips to him.

Dante obliged, trailing kisses along her cheek.

"There is another reason, a less romantic one," he uttered on a heavy sigh.

Anastasia searched his eyes. Fine lines framed the perimeter. The weight and responsibility of being an earl had already begun to wear on him. She hoped that she could bring some of the joy back into his life.

"My grandmother is intent on ruining my aunt and cousin. If I do not announce my choice of bride this evening she will carry out her threat. Although my aunt is not concerned with what gossip my grandmother might stir, I am. Aunt Ursula and my cousin do not deserve my grandmother's wrath."

"Why do you let her dictate your life?" Dante was a strong man, capable of so much, except where his grandmother was concerned.

"After you," Dante sucked in a deep breath. She felt him struggle with the words. "I did not care about anything. My grandmother has a knack for dictating to the family, especially the men of my family. Perhaps I learned to acquiesce by example. Regardless, I never felt the need to stand up to her schemes until now. I will marry you, protect my aunt and cousin, and not let my grandmother disrupt our happiness." He kissed her lips, sealing his vow.

She reached up on her tiptoes and kissed him. "I think it is a wonderful plan."

There was still one unpleasantness looming that Anastasia must tell him. They could not build a future without him knowing the whole truth of what happened.

Anastasia was trying to muster the courage to tell him but the feel of his lips on her neck was most distracting. And his hand, oh lord, how she missed the feel of his hand on her body. A tingling that started where his lips touched her skin travelled all the way down to her toes. She leaned into him. His hand roamed down her body, cupping her bottom. She gasped with that movement, but did not push him away. Anastasia did not want the moment to end.

Dante moved his hand to her waist while the other took her hand in his and began to waltz. She rested her head against his chest. The sound of his rapid beating heart set the rhythm for their dance. They waltzed through the marble gallery, circling Greek goddesses and Roman putti.

"My Anna, how I've missed you." He brushed a kiss across her cheek. "I have always loved you."

Anastasia raised her head, and when her eyes met his, she knew that there was no place she would rather be than in his arms. As he twirled her around a winged goddess, she reached up and kissed his lips. She may have initiated the kiss, but it quickly turned into a mutual dance of desire.

Dante guided her past a reclining Venus, twirling her through the space. Anastasia had never been so happy, but there was a dark shadow waiting to extinguish that happiness. There was something that she had to confess before they could marry.

Anastasia took in a deep breath to steady her nerves. She needed to tell him everything…right now. "There is something I need to tell you."

"Anastasia, it's time," Isabel voice ricocheted against the marble walls.

She had finally mustered the courage to tell him and just like that, the opportunity was gone.

* * *

Having Anna so near was truly inspirational. Dante could not wait to enter his studio and begin the new painting that his imagination conjured while dancing with her just a short time ago. If it weren't meant to be a surprise, he would have insisted that Anna joined him at the cottage. But then again, he wasn't sure that he would have been able to focus on painting.

Dante left the pantheon and traversed the long way about. It felt good to walk in the warm afternoon sun. He picked up several small rocks and threw them one by one across the water, watching as they skipped along the surface before dropping into the clear depths. For the first time in a long time, he was content with life. He continued on his journey. By the time he reached the cottage, the inspiration that had begun at the pantheon had grown, the image secure in his mind.

Without wasting time, he prepared the canvas and paints, and set to work on what would be his wedding present to his Anna. Images of a distant cottage came to mind. The pathway lined with all her favorite flowers perfectly in bloom. He remembered when she had told him that she had wanted to live in that cottage one day. It was the first day they met, the day he fell in love with her. They would never live in that cottage, but he hoped that this painting would make up for that.

Several hours had passed before Dante realized that he best put down his paints and retreat to the main house. The final ball was this evening. Glancing at the image taking shape on the canvas, he was pleased with his work for the day.

* * *

Dante walked with determination toward his grandmother's private sitting room. This was the moment he had been dreading all day, but it had to be done. He knocked on the door and waited to be admitted. Dabney came to the door and without word, stepped aside to allow Dante entrance.

"Grandmother, I've come to inform you of my decision." He tried to keep his voice firm, in control.

His grandmother sat poised in her favorite chair, waiting for him to speak.

The eloquent speech he had prepared to convince his grandmother that this was his life, his choice, vanished beneath unsteady nerves. "Miss Anastasia Quintin." He said her name with conviction.

Her features were impossible to read and rarely seemed to change. She took in a slow, steady breath before a shallow smile crossed her face. "If she will have you, then I suppose I cannot object."

For reasons he could not explain, his grandmother's words had not set well with him. But before he could question her, she dismissed him. "I must finish preparing for this evening." She stood from her chair, crossed the room and disappeared into her chamber, leaving a confused Dante wondering what she was up to now.

Chapter Twelve

"That shade of blue is quite becoming on you." Philippa said as Anastasia entered their shared sitting room. "You look positively radiant."

"I feel…happy." Ever since Dante had proposed, she could not keep the smile from her face. Never in her wildest dreams would she have imagined that she would be a countess, married to her one true love and live in a grand house such as this.

Sadness still loomed in her heart, and probably always would, but at least the past was now at peace. There was still one detail that she had yet to tell Dante, but she had yet to work up the courage to reveal why her father had sent her away. Every time she came close to explaining, something or someone interrupted.

"I'm glad. You deserve happiness."

Anastasia eyed Philippa, suspecting that her dear friend had more to do with her current state than she was willing to say. "Perhaps one day you will tell me your role in all this."

Philippa gave Anastasia a sly little smile. "I only did what was necessary."

Just then, Isabel entered the room, handkerchief in hand and looking rather sullen.

"Are you crying?" Philippa tilted her head in question.

"No, I don't cry. I just fear…that I am losing Anastasia forever." This was as close as Isabel came to dramatics.

"Oh, my dearest, you are not losing me." Anastasia strolled up to Isabel and took her hands in hers and squeezed them with reassurance. "We will still be the best of friends. Distance and an earl could never come between us."

"Promise?"

"I promise." She ended her oath with a kiss on Isabel's cheek. "Come, let's finish getting ready."

It seemed as if only a couple of minutes had passed before there was a knock on the door. Philippa went to answer and was greeted by Dabney. "Lord Huntingdon has requested Miss Quintin's presence before the evening festivities begin."

Anastasia and Philippa both squealed with girlish delight. One more quick check in the mirror and Anastasia left the room, following Dabney. She still did not care for the servant and hoped that after she married, Dabney would treat her with more respect. She doubted that would be the case.

"This way, Miss Quintin." Anastasia followed the sour-faced woman. She was not going to let Dabney's bitterness ruin the evening.

Anastasia relished in the excitement that was bubbling inside. She hardly noticed her surroundings, too lost in the thoughts of Dante. Several minutes passed before she realized she had no idea what part of the house she was in. Anastasia suspected she was now in the family wing.

"You may wait in the pink sitting room for Lord Huntingdon. He will be along momentarily."

Anastasia entered the sitting room, which seemed far too feminine to be a place where a gentleman would retreat. She looked about the space and noticed lace doilies, ornate pillows in every shade of pink imaginable, and several delicate music boxes. Where was she?

"Good evening, Miss Quintin." Lady Huntingdon's calm voice sent shivers down her spine.

She swallowed the hard lump in her throat. "Good evening, Lady Huntingdon. I…I was waiting for…"

"My grandson will not be attending us." Lady Huntingdon walked out of the shadows and took her seat at a large mulberry damask chair. "It was I who summoned you. Please have a seat."

Anastasia did not want to oblige. In fact, all she wanted to do was run from the room. Unfortunately, Dabney was blocking the only way out of the room. Lady Huntingdon's eyes bore into her, awaiting her request to be fulfilled. She sat down on the edge of the elegant sofa and clasped her hands in her lap.

The silence lingered on as Lady Huntingdon inspected Anastasia. When she finally spoke, Lady Huntingdon wasted no time with pleasantries and got straight to the point.

"I know your secret."

If it were possible, Anastasia thought her heart stopped beating. There was only one secret that she could be referring to and Lady Huntingdon could not possibly know about her baby. She did not know what to say. Anything she said could be strewed. She jumped to her feet, hoping the opportunity to escape would present itself.

Lady Huntingdon stood and then circled around her like a vulture eyeing a carcass. "I know that you had a summer romance with my grandson." She was standing behind Anastasia and whispered into her ear. "I know that you wanted to marry him." She came around stood directly in front of her now. "I know that you claimed to have been pregnant with his child."

Oh, no! Panic seized Anastasia. How did she…?

"Oh, yes," Lady Huntingdon hissed out the words like they brought her great pleasure. "I know *all* about the two of you. It is quite unfortunate that you were sent away to have that bastard. Mercifully *it* died."

"How dare you," Anastasia screamed. "My daughter wasn't a bastard. Dante said he would marry me and instead…" She choked on the tears as the painful lump in her throat choked off her words.

"How dare I?" Lady Huntingdon remained eerily calm. "I was not going to take any chance that some fortune hunter of inferior birth was going to infiltrate my family and cause scandal. Oh, yes, I knew all about you. Who do you think intercepted your thoughtful letters?" The sarcasm in Lady Huntingdon's tone of voice hurt just as much as the words she spoke.

"You kept us apart?" Anastasia could not believe what she was hearing. How could one woman be so cruel?

"Yes, and fortunate for me, your father wanted to be rid of you just as much as I did. Although I would never have guessed that he would have told everyone you died. I understand the funeral was quite lovely and well attended."

Anastasia felt as if she had been slapped in the face. She had always known that her father had not cared for her the way he cared for her brothers, but to treat her with such disdain was incomprehensible. Anastasia could feel the life being sucked out of her with each breath Lady Huntingdon took.

"What is that you want from me?"

"I want you to leave and never see or write to my grandson ever again."

"But we…"

"What could my grandson possibly gain by having you as a wife?" The words pierced her heart. She did not want to marry him because he was an earl. Title had never been important to her.

"We love each other and that should…"

"Love is not a requirement in my world. Breeding and lineage are far more important than love." She spat out the last words as if they were poison on her tongue. Anastasia was about to argue that there was nothing greater than love when Lady Huntingdon continued her assault. "What do you think will happen when the *ton* learns that your family disowned you after you had an illicit affair? You, some commoner who at seventeen schemed and faked your own death so no one would ever know the truth."

Anastasia was going to be sick. Dozens of thoughts raced through her mind, but the words failed to reach her mouth.

"And what of Miss Albryght?" Despite the nausea rising, Anastasia was able to speak with some force. "She has nothing to do with this."

"No?" Lady Huntingdon's glare suggested otherwise. This woman would stop at nothing to achieve her goals. "Isn't it Miss Albryght and her bastard of a half brother, Mr. Weston, who took you in?" She circled around Anastasia again. "I'm sure Mr. Weston was an attentive benefactor for all those years."

Anger flared through her veins. "There was nothing ever untoward. Weston is like a brother to me. Stop twisting the facts." Anastasia could not contain the anger or her breathing. Her chest rose and fell. Her head ached with all the turmoil. She had finally found her happily ever after, and now Lady Huntingdon was ripping it from her.

"Your father will attest to your trickery."

"My father? I haven't seen him in eight years."

With nonchalance Lady Huntingdon said, "He is easily swayed for a minimal price."

It was a shock to hear how little her family valued her. "What is it that you want? Do you honestly believe that these games will force Dante to abandon me?"

Lady Huntingdon waved her hand at Anastasia to stop her from speaking. "I have made arrangements with a friend for you to have a position as a lady's companion in Scotland. You leave at dawn tomorrow." She looked hard at Anastasia. "As you can see, I am not an unreasonable person."

"Not unreasonable? For the second time, and I suspect more, you are trying to ruin my life. Well, it is not up to you. Dante will never allow you to do this." Although she tried to speak with conviction, her words had no impact on Lady Huntingdon's resolve.

"Ah, I see. Still determined to fight for what you believe is true love." Lady Huntingdon's gaze turned harsh. "It doesn't exist, Miss Quintin. It is a silly schoolgirl notion that is shattered the moment…" Her words trailed off. Anastasia suspected that years ago Lady Huntingdon had suffered her own heartache that shaped the woman standing before her.

Anastasia thought to appeal to her, woman to woman. "Surely you can…"

Lady Huntingdon waved her hand to silence Anastasia. It was a gesture that she was quickly coming to dislike.

"I'm sure Miss Albryght would be most interested to hear how you destroyed her season before she even had one. And then there is Mr. Weston and his new bride. Scandal seems to follow Mrs. Weston." Lady Huntingdon paused and then added with sarcasm, "I am sure she will rise above the gossip."

Anastasia could not believe what she was hearing. Lady Huntingdon was prepared to destroy others' lives just to get what she wanted. Dante had mentioned that his grandmother cared for no one save herself and now Anastasia was witnessing it firsthand.

"Oh, and let's not forget Dante's aunt and cousin. I'm sure he would still love you even after you ruined their lives."

She had to get away from Lady Huntingdon. "You're insane," Anastasia said as she backed away from Lady Huntingdon. The pounding of her heart clouded her thoughts. The moment she spoke the words, she knew she had made a grievous mistake. "When Dante hears what you've done…"

Lady Huntingdon stepped in closer to Anastasia. "I had a feeling that you would put up an argument." She waved her hand, signaling someone, but before Anastasia could react, a firm hand covered mouth, and then her world went dark.

* * *

Anastasia felt numb from the cold. The pounding in her head was a steady staccato that would not ease. The last thing she remembered was arguing with Lady Huntingdon. She had not even seen who approached from behind.

She glanced about the dark room. A window, no wider than the length of her arm, let in a soft stream of moonlight. She had no idea where she was, but the howling of the wind sent shivers down her spine. With wobbling legs, Anastasia managed to stand, but quickly lurched forward as what felt like thousands of needles pierced her legs. She bent over, rubbing her legs, trying to relieve the pain. When the stinging lessened, she hobbled over to the window and glanced outside.

She was in the tower that Isabel had told her about on the journey to Paradiso. Looking down into the dark depths below, she suspected she was fairly high up. Even if she screamed for help, she was too far from the main house for anyone to hear her. She had to discover a way out of here. What lies would Lady Huntingdon weave to try and convince Dante she left him? No, he would never believe his grandmother, but what horrors did she have in store for Anastasia?

Anastasia wanted to cry. The tears were already pooling in the corner of her eyes, but she would not allow them to spill. First she had to escape, and then she could cry. When she was safe in Dante's arms, then she *would* cry.

From what she could discern, the interior space was spartan. She ran her hand along the wall until she reached the door, fumbled to find the handle then pulled with all her might. The moment the door swung open, she knew she was in trouble.

"And where do you think you're going?" She knew that voice. Dabney.

"Why am I here?"

"Lady Huntingdon wants to ensure that you will not cause any problems when Lord Huntingdon announces his bride."

Anastasia glanced about and a plan formed in her mind. She did not know if it would work, but she had nothing to lose.

"Lady Huntingdon's plan will not succeed." Distracting Dabney with conversation, Anastasia began to walk back toward the open door. "Lord Huntingdon will not be fooled again by his grandmother."

"Little do you know about men. Money and a pretty face can sway their fickle hearts." Dabney continued to talk about men's fickle ways as Anastasia edged up to the door. She was hoping that the dark room hid her actions from Dabney. Clasping her hand around the handle, she waited.

Anastasia baited the servant. She didn't know what she was saying but wanted her to close the distance. "I don't believe that Lord Huntingdon's heart is fickle. I think you had your heart broken."

"You're wrong." Dabney growled out as she took a step toward Anastasia. "I broke his heart. I left him." The room may have been dark, but Anastasia could sense that Dabney was dangerous. The woman scurried toward Anastasia. "You need a lesson in manners." Before Dabney could touch her, Anastasia pulled the door back and swung it toward the belligerent servant with all her might.

A loud thwack echoed against the walls and then Dabney slumped onto the floor. Anastasia was breathing heavy. Her heart practically jumped out of her chest.

Lifting up her skirts, Anastasia hurried from the room. Everything was dark all around her, except for the narrow streams of moonlight penetrating through the windows. With caution, Anastasia hurried down the steps, one hand on the wall, the other on the railing as she circled her way down the tower.

By the time she reached the bottom, she was out of breath, but she could not give up. At the bottom, she yanked on the door, but it did not budge. Those tears that she had managed to keep at bay were threatening again. "Not now," she commanded her emotions to obey.

She pulled on the door again and again. Frustration rose with each tug. She leaned her head against the cool wood door trying to think of a way out of this predicament.

Turning around, she slammed her body against the door. *Damn.* She looked up and noticed a wider stream of light coming from the floor above. Anastasia made her way up the stairs and entered the room. A small alcove with a window wider than in the upper room was off to one side. She went to the glassless window. The cool night air rushed past her, the sound of a tree branch scraping against the side of the tower startled her. She looked out the window. It was still quite a drop, but she thought she could make it.

Sounds from above ricocheted down the tower. "Where are you?" an angry voice demanded, getting closer.

Anastasia looked around for something she could use as a weapon, but the room was empty.

She was trapped.

Her body started to tremble. All sorts of morbid thoughts raced through her mind.

"I know you're here." Dabney's voice edged closer.

Anastasia did not stop and think if what she was about to do was a good idea or not. Bracing herself against the window she inhaled deeply and then screamed out into the dark and silent night. "Help me!" She took in another deep breath. "I'm in the tower."

"That wasn't too smart of you." Dabney's voice was right behind Anastasia, and sent a chill down her spine. Her head snapped up. Demon-like eyes met hers.

"Help me!" She turned and continued to scream, praying that someone might hear her. She inhaled and prepared to scream again. She heard Dabney approach before she felt the woman's icy cold hands on her body.

Anastasia glanced about. There was nowhere for her to go. "Please don't do this," she cried.

Dabney did not say a word, but laughed in a garish sort of way as she lunged toward Anastasia, forcing part of her body out the window.

"Please don't," Anastasia pleaded again. Her heart was pounding against her chest as the fear took hold. She stared into the dark abyss below, fighting for control. "Help me," she screamed into the night as her body began to slip further out the window. "Someone help me!"

Chapter Thirteen

Dante was anxious. And for reasons he could not state. He should have been ecstatic. Tonight was the night that he announced to the world that Anna was his bride. She was the only woman he had ever wanted. He could not shake the feeling that something was about to happen, and it was nothing good. The last time he felt this way, he thought he had lost her forever.

The white cravat his valet had elegantly tied was suffocating. Dante had been dressed for the ball well ahead of any of the guests and rather than loiter in his room, he went to his study. He would have preferred the cottage. At least there, he could complete the painting he had started for Anastasia.

He poured a glass of brandy, noticing his hand shook with anxious nervousness as he swirled the contents. His grandmother had taken the news of his choice in bride well—too well. Perhaps that was what was bothering him.

He downed the contents in one gulp. The liquid burned his throat as it travelled into the empty pit of his stomach. The anxiety had not eased. He reached for the decanter again. Before he had a chance to pour another hearty helping, the door to his study flew open, crashing against the wall.

"Where is she?" Mr. Weston demanded. Dante had met the man on several occasions, was familiar with his work as investigator to the *ton*, but had never interacted much with him on a personal level.

"Your sister?" Why was he being questioned about Miss Albryght?

"No, Miss Quintin." Weston stormed up to him, and grabbed him by the cravat. "If any harm comes to her…"

"Weston, stop!" Mrs. Weston screamed from the open doorway.

"Give me one good reason," he said over his shoulder, but was still glaring at Dante.

"You don't have all the facts." At least Mrs. Weston was a voice of reason. Although Dante was unsure what facts she could be referring to. He knew he had done nothing wrong.

"What do you want with Miss Quintin?"

Weston pulled him in close, twisting Dante's cravat. "I'm here to take her home."

The breath was caught in his throat, but he continued to hold his ground. He pushed off Weston and ground out with a rasp, "Like hell you will. Who gives you the right…?"

"She is under my protection. I will not see her hurt and abandoned like she was eight years ago."

Weston threw a punch that landed square on Dante's jaw with a loud *thwack*. Pain ricocheted through his face.

"Stop this!" Mrs. Weston screamed as she ran between them.

Dante lifted his head, rubbing his jaw. His head was spinning. "What the bloody hell is this all about?"

Speaking over his wife, Weston growled out, "Your grandmother didn't think the baby was yours. Did you think the same? Is that why you sent her away this evening when she told you? You couldn't accept the truth."

Baby?

"Baby?" Mrs. Weston managed to utter the word first.

When Mr. Weston failed to answer, Dante asked the same question. "Baby? What baby?"

Weston stepped in close. He looked like he wanted to kill someone. He narrowed his gaze and searched deep into Dante's eyes. He would have been scared if he had something to hide; the man had intimidation down to a science.

"You mean to tell me that you know nothing of your daughter?"

Dante stumbled back.

"Daughter?" *He had a daughter?*

He tried to formulate the words when Weston continued to enlighten him. "You never knew that Anastasia had borne and lost a baby eight years ago?"

Dante was about to demand a complete explanation when Miss Albryght pushed her way into the room. "Lord Huntingdon, Anastasia is missing."

The burning in his throat thickened. The fire in his stomach exploded. "What do you mean she is missing?" he asked as he pulled away from Weston's grasp.

"Anastasia left her room over an hour ago and was coming to see you." Miss Albryght skirted past her brother. "But Lybbe overheard Gibbs tell Dabney that the carriage would take Anastasia to Scotland first thing in the morning."

The dread that had been simmering in his gut was now at a full boil.

"Where do you think you're going?" Weston demanded as Dante pushed past him.

"To find my future wife." He did not wait for Weston's response or to see if anyone was going to follow him. He stormed to his grandmother's sitting room and entered without knocking.

"Where is she?" There was no doubt in his mind that his grandmother was behind this.

"To whom are you referring?" she said with a sly smile that only confirmed his suspicions.

"Miss Quintin. Where is Miss Quintin?"

"I have no idea. Although Dabney said she saw the young lady in question leave in such a hurry earlier this afternoon."

"She's lying." The accusation came from behind Dante. He turned around to see Weston reclining against the doorjamb.

For as long as Dante could remember everyone had folded to Grandmother's demands, but no more. This was going to end tonight.

"What do you know of the baby?"

Grandmother's face paled, but her features remained stoic. "I have no idea what you are referring to." She ignored Dante and continued on with her embroidery. It was an odd task at a moment such as this, but Dante suspected it was her means to ignore his questions.

Weston stormed further into the room. "Dammit to hell. You are the one responsible for hurting Anastasia." Dante stopped Weston before he could reach his grandmother. She did not deserve his protection, but he still needed to know to where Anastasia had disappeared, and yelling at his grandmother was not going to achieve results.

Dante rounded on the bitter old woman and leaned on the table, blocking her view of herself in the mirror. "Is it true that there was a baby and that you knew it was mine?"

"It could have been any man's bastard. Miss Quintin's father knew who you were even if she claimed she did not. I wasn't going to take any chances."

Dante slammed his fist down on the table, rattling the expensive decorative glass bottles. "What did you do?" His voice reverberated through the space. It was the first time in his life that he had raised such a forceful voice to any woman, let alone his grandmother.

She raised her muted brown eyes to his. "I did what I needed to do to preserve the appearance of this family. That little whore…"

He whipped his grandmother around to face him. "How dare you play with people's lives like it is a game of chess." Dante had lost all patience. If she were a man, Dante would have punched her by now. "Where is she? Tell me where Anastasia is or I'll…"

"You'll what?" She stared at him, daring him. "You can threaten me all you want, but I am still mistress of Paradiso."

To say that Dante was frustrated would have been an understatement. Although his grandmother was responsible for Anna's disappearance, among other things, she was not about to reveal anything. Grandmother would be as silent as the grave just to spite him. How was he…? He turned to Weston. "Help me find her."

Weston nodded his head and then turned in the direction of the hall and spoke to someone. "Be sure that she doesn't leave this room, Bacheler."

Weston then turned his attention back to Dante. "This is your estate. Tell me everywhere she could possibly be."

Laughter broke through his thoughts. "You'll never find her." His grandmother's final words sent an icy chill down his spine.

Dante guided Mr. Weston in the hall and the ladies followed. The man Mr. Weston referred to as Bacheler brushed past them and entered his grandmother's sitting room.

As if answering the unspoken question, Mr. Weston said, "Bacheler has been in my employ for many years. He can be trusted."

"Your man understands not to let her go?"

"Don't worry about Bacheler." Dante heard the annoyed tone lacing Mr. Weston's words and chose to ignore it.

"I'll concern myself with whatever…"

Mrs. Weston interjected before Dante could finish his sentence. "Is it possible for the two of you to stop acting like little children? We have more important matters to resolve."

"I don't believe Lady Huntingdon would have locked Anastasia away in the house," Miss Albryght began in a firm tone. "But, Philippa and I can search here just in case. I'm sure we can get some of the guests to help."

"Good, you two start searching." Before Mr. Weston let the ladies leave, he pulled Mrs. Weston toward him. "Good evening my dear," he said before he gave his wife a hearty kiss.

"Really, Weston," Miss Albryght exclaimed. "Could that not wait till after Anastasia is safe?"

Mr. Weston did not say a word, just smiled.

There were several places Anna could be. "Why don't we start with the pantheon?"

"We will rendezvous in thirty minutes," Weston instructed his wife and Miss Albryght. "And be careful."

"Let's go." Dante took off at a clipped pace with Mr. Weston on his heels.

They searched the pantheon, the cottage, and even the grotto, but there was no sign of Anna anywhere.

"Damn," Dante swore under his breath. "Where could she be?"

"There must be someplace else that Lady Huntingdon could have had her taken." The frustration in Mr. Weston's tone matched his own.

There was one location that Dante had not thought of at first. "Bloody hell, the tower." He began to run in that direction, with Mr. Weston close behind. It had not been used in years and since it was not visible from the house or temple, it was an ideal place for Anna to be kept captive. He had no doubt in his mind that she was being held against her will.

As he neared the clearing, Dante thought he heard a shriek in the distance. He stopped, trying to get a better listen, but his heart pounded so loudly in his chest it disturbed the night's sounds.

Weston came up beside him. "It's Anastasia."

Without another word, they started running in the direction of the cry. When the tower came into view, Dante's heart stopped. Anna was dangling from a window twenty feet off the ground, her pale blue gown flapping in the wind.

"Help me!" Her panicked cry set Dante's nerves over the edge.

They ran toward her. "Hang on," he called out to her, unsure if she heard him over her pleas.

A female figure was struggling to push Anna further out the window. The clouds cleared overhead, casting light on the dire situation.

Dante ran with every bit of energy he possessed, only slowing as he reached the tower door. He yanked on the heavy handle, but the door was locked.

"I'll get the door open. You go to Anastasia." Dante did not care if Weston ordered him about. Right now all that mattered was Anastasia. He wanted her safe and in his arms.

Dante was standing directly beneath her, but there was nothing he could do. He felt helpless. "I'm right here, Anna." He called up to her. "Just hang on."

"I can't," she cried. He could hear the anguish in her voice. Dante ran a frustrated hand through his hair. He had to save her.

Out of the corner of his eye, he saw Weston ramming the door with his shoulder. The sound of wood cracking broke through Anna's cries. Another charge and Weston disappeared into the tower. After that, everything happened quickly.

Loud shouts penetrated through the tower.

Cries and commotion in the distance grew closer.

Anna screamed for help, her hands fumbling to hang on.

In the next moment, Dante watched as she lost her grip. All thought of himself disappeared. He braced himself to catch her. He would take the brunt of the fall.

Cries echoed through the countryside as her body slammed into his. Dante wrapped his arms around her as he fell to the ground.

Anna was sobbing heavily, her chest heaving with each breath she took. Brushing her hair out of her face, he kissed her cheek. "Are you all right?" He ran his hands over her body. Miraculously she didn't appear to have broken anything.

"I'm...I'm...yes." She was breathing heavily.

"Shh, I've got you." Dante sat up; a swift pain lanced his back as he cradled her in his arms. "Nothing and no one can harm you." She buried her head into his chest and cried softly.

As if on cue, the woman partly responsible for Anna's current predicament was guided out of the tower by Weston. He looked over at them. "Anastasia, are you all right?"

Her breathing had evened to a steady calm. "Yes. Thank you for coming, Weston."

Jealousy reared its ugly head. Why did Weston get her appreciation and he did not? Surely she was not going to blame him for his grandmother's actions?

"I'm going to take this one up to the house," Weston said as he nudged Dabney along. The woman's face looked bruised. He didn't want to know what Weston had done, but was thankful for his assistance.

Anna turned her attention to Dante. "Thank you for catching me." She kissed his cheek and then rested her head against his shoulder. The jealous beast disappeared.

"You are most welcome."

"How did you find me?"

"Miss Albryght alerted us to your disappearance. I questioned my grandmother."

"Your grandmother hates me." Anna shook her head. "I don't know what I ever did to earn such disdain, but..." He saw the tears pool in her eyes. "She kept us apart."

Perhaps it was too soon to discuss the baby, but he needed to know. "Why didn't you tell me?"

She stilled in his arms, but did not look up at him. She must have guessed to what he was referring. "I wanted to, but it just hurt too much. She was so small and weak." That final sentence brought on more tears.

Dante raised his Anna's chin and looked into her eyes. His heart mourned for the daughter he had not known he had lost. He would never forgive himself for not being there for either of them. "I'm so sorry that I was not there."

"I used to blame you. I thought that you didn't care. I was so hurt and angry."

Shaking her head, she sniffed back the tears. "But, you didn't know." She stroked his cheek. "I cannot be angry now, knowing what I do. I just want you, Dante."

Reaching up, she pulled his head down and took his lips in a soft kiss.

"Anastasia!" The sound of Miss Albryght's cries broke through the calm as she came running toward them, followed closely behind by Mrs. Weston.

Dante began to stand, his back reminding him that he took the brunt of Anna's fall. At the sight of her friend running toward them, Anna hobbled forward.

Miss Albryght almost knocked Anna over she embraced her with such force. "Oh, you're all right. I thought..."

"You're not crying, Isabel?"

"I never cry," she responded through sniffles just as Mrs. Weston approached.

"Oh, Anastasia," Mrs. Weston started encircling both Anna and Miss Albryght in her embrace. "Thank heavens you are safe."

Anna reached her hand out to Dante. She did not say a word, and she didn't have to. Her loving touch said it all.

* * *

By the time they reached the house, the guests had already gathered in the ballroom. The sound of the orchestra playing invited them into the festive space. Despite all that had happened, there was great cause for celebration this evening. However, before he could celebrate, there was one unpleasant but much overdue task Dante must oversee.

"I need to speak with my grandmother alone, but I don't want you far away. Will you wait outside the sitting room?"

Dante wanted to confront his grandmother and if Anna was with him, he suspected the old tyrant would not cooperate even more than usual.

"I'll be right here." Anna brushed a kiss on his cheek.

Dante strolled into the sitting room. After this evening, he would have no further contact with his grandmother.

"Is it true?" He demanded as he stood over his grandmother.

She did not even try to hide her annoyance at being confined, and now with being interrogated. "Is what true?"

"Let me refresh your memory." Dante continued to hold his ground. It felt good. "That you purposely kept Anastasia and I apart. That you knew she was with my child." The fear and guilt shone bright in her eyes, but her features maintained an eerie calm. "That even after her family informed me of her passing, you knew it not to be true. That you paid her father to lie for you."

Not admitting her guilt, she stated, "Whatever you claimed that I have done was for the good of this family. Your grandfather did not understand that; why should I expect you to?"

Dante suspected his grandmother was responsible for far more than just keeping him and Anastasia apart. Over the years, there had been too many accidents, too many mysterious happenings to be coincidental.

He knew his grandmother would not confess. Drastic measures were the only solution to this disaster. "You are forthwith excluded from any and all doings with this family. I am the Earl of Huntingdon and I will be making the decisions from now on."

"You cannot do this." Her voice remained calm, unaffected, but the fear in her eyes spoke otherwise.

"It is already decided. Arrangements will be made for you to be taken to Hunt Hall. You will not leave the estate, host no events, and receive no visitors." It was the most secluded estate he owned, not to mention the only one that had yet to be renovated.

"So I am to be exiled for one simple mistake."

"Simple?" Dante's voice escalated. "You tried to ruin my life. You wanted to harm Anastasia because she did not fit into your scheme."

"What did you expect? She was the daughter of a curate, and you were the grandson of an earl. There were appearances to be kept. I was not going to have my family's lineage be tainted by some...some nobody."

Dante could not believe that everything his grandmother had done was because of title and station. "Is that all you care about?"

Grandmother remained still, refusing to answer or even acknowledge him.

There was no point in arguing. No matter what he said, no matter how hard he tried to reason with her, she would always see herself as being correct, justified in her actions. "I am done discussing this." He turned his back on her. "From this day forth, I have no grandmother."

She did not say a word, or even express any remorse. He should have known. Had he opened his eyes a little wider, he would have seen the truth of her long ago. The only person for whom she had ever shown any affection was his uncle—her first-born. And even then, her affection came with a price.

Dante would not let her dictate to him anymore.

For the first time in his life, he was his own man.

Epilogue

"Don't you think the guests will wonder where the bride and groom have gone off to?" Anastasia teased as Dante clicked the reins, driving them further away from the main house.

"It is our wedding day and we should be able to do whatever we want. Besides, the wedding breakfast was almost over and I want to be alone with you."

Anastasia did not know where Dante was taking her, and she didn't care. All that mattered was that she was married to her one true love and was finally alone with her husband.

Husband. Her entire body tingled with delight over that one word. She could not keep the smile from her face. It was a most perfect summer day. It was as if the sun shone just for them, that the birds sang a song inspired by their love.

"What are you thinking about, my lady?"

She had always loved when he used that endearment. "Just how blissfully happy I am."

He leaned in, kissed her cheek, and whispered, "It is only the beginning."

They had agreed to not discuss their previous sorrows. Perhaps one day they could revisit all that had happened, but for now, they wanted to live for each other and focus on building their future.

Dante brought the curricle to a halt. A groom rushed from out of nowhere to take the reins. "When did you plan this?"

He did not answer but gave her that sideways smile that had always melted her heart. He offered his hand in assistance. "Shall we?"

They had stopped in front of a well-maintained cottage. During the few times Anastasia had been able to explore the estate over the past several weeks, she had never come across this sweet little place.

"Where are we?"

"My grandfather had this built shortly after he married my grandmother. I suspect it was his hideaway. She only ventured here once while he was alive. After he died, she had tried on a number of occasions to arrange for it to be torn down, but my uncle would never allow it."

Purple and pink orchids lined the cobbled path that led to the cottage door. Anastasia was transported to another time and place, to a little cottage that a small girl had dreamed about living in one day.

Dante opened the door and escorted her inside. The bright white interior sparkled like a new bauble. It was nothing like the cottage she imagined. This was far better. Instead of a sitting room or parlor, it looked as if an artist's studio had been set up. White canvases of varying sizes lined one of the walls. An easel draped with a cloth stood in the center of the room. A small woodpile was neatly stacked was off to one side.

"I wanted to give you your wedding present." Dante placed his hand in the small of her back and guided her toward the easel. "Close your eyes."

Anastasia gave him a sideways glance before obeying. She felt the wisp of air brush over her as he pulled the cloth away. The fresh scent of soap tickled her senses as Dante rejoined her.

"Open your eyes," he whispered just before kissing her ear.

"Oh, my," she breathed heavily. "It's my cottage." She stepped in to look closer. Every detail was as she remembered; the only difference was that he had not portrayed the dilapidation. Instead, he depicted what she had told him it would look like after she restored it. "After all these years, you remembered what it looked like?"

Dante was beside her. "I have to confess. I had started the sketches eight years ago."

She turned to face him. Her eyes locked on his. She had often dreamed of moments like this when they had first met, and she held those memories close for all these years.

Her heart swelled with a joy she didn't think was possible.

"I knew I loved you the moment I saw you."

"And I you, Lady Huntingdon."

ABOUT THE AUTHOR

Alanna Lucas is a historical romance author who loves writing historical romance just as much as she loves reading it. When not daydreaming of her next hero, Alanna can be found spending time with a book, her family, or plotting her next travel destination.

Alanna is a member of the Romance Writers of America, East Valley Authors, The Beau Monde, and Celtic Hearts Romance Writers. She makes her home in Southern California with her family. She loves to hear from readers.

Did you enjoy this book? Drop us a line and say so! We love to hear from readers, and so do our authors. To connect, visit www.boroughspublishinggroup.com online, send comments directly to info@boroughspublishinggroup.com, or friend us on Facebook and Twitter. And be sure to check back regularly for contests and new releases in your favorite subgenres of romance!

Are you an aspiring writer? Check out www.boroughspublishinggroup.com/submit and see if we can help you make your dreams come true.

Made in the USA
San Bernardino, CA
24 March 2016